THE FEUD IN THE CHALET SCHOOL

THE FEUD IN THE CHALET SCHOOL

ELINOR M. BRENT-DYER

Armada

First published in the U.K.
by W. & R. Chambers Ltd, Edinburgh.
First published in Armada
in 1986 by Fontana Paperbacks,
8 Grafton Street, London W1X 3LA.

Armada is an imprint of
Fontana Paperbacks, a division of
the Collins Publishing Group

Printed in Great Britain by
William Collins Sons & Co. Ltd, Glasgow.

To Mary
With love from Elinor

CONTENTS

Chapter 1

THE BEGINNING OF IT

IF Miss Holroyd had never decided to move her school; if some careless idiot had not tossed a smouldering cigarette-end on to the grass that was dry as tinder; if Miriam Ashley had been a person of humbler mind and less obstinacy; if, above all, the Middles hadn't been like most Middles, young demons when roused, this story would not have been written.

It all began a year before, when Miss Holroyd finally decided to start a school in Switzerland for girls whose parents could not afford the fees of the expensive finishing schools, but who would be glad if their daughters might have two or three terms abroad with special attention to languages.

It was not a sudden decision. Bethia Holroyd had pondered the idea for some years before an unexpected legacy from a great-uncle made everything possible. It would mean starting in a comparatively small way, but that was what she had always expected. For one more year she remained in her post as head of the languages department in a big boarding school, spending all her holidays in Switzerland hunting for somewhere to start. She finally obtained a year's lease on a house on the shore of Lake Geneva. And there she went when Queen Elfrida's broke up for the summer holidays, taking with her the good wishes of her former colleagues; a handsome clock, the gift of her pupils; a certainty of fifteen girls as a beginning; and a widowed cousin who had agreed to share in the adventure as Matron and housekeeper.

Edith Kent, a friend who had taught English in a secondary school, was coming as English mistress and, for mathematics and games, she had secured the services of Miriam Ashley, who had been the very capable Head Prefect at Queen Elfrida's eight years previously and since then had collected a degree at London University and four years' experience in teaching in a south coast school. Other subjects were to be taught by visiting staff for the moment. Later, if her project proved a success, Miss Holroyd hoped to take a larger place and then she would dispense as far as possible with visiting mistresses.

St Hilda's prospered from the first. Miss Holroyd herself was an excellent teacher. In her own line, so was Miss Kent who, however, showed an inclination to slip out of any big responsibilities outside her work. That was more than made up for by Miriam Ashley. She loved responsibility—the more and the bigger the better! That young woman had a high opinion of her own capabilities. Miss Kent was supposed to be Senior Mistress, but Miss Ashley speedily usurped most of the work. Bethia Holroyd kept her firmly in her place over things that mattered. Miriam was young and would presently learn a little more humility when she had had more experience. Meanwhile, as things were, it did no harm, and in other ways she was an excellent colleague.

The first two terms went well. More pupils came for the Easter term, and when St Hilda's reassembled for the summer, the school had grown to twenty-seven and there was already promise of more girls for the second year. Summer, however, showed one drawback with which Miss Holroyd had forgotten to reckon—the heat. Switzerland sweltered under a heatwave for almost the whole of June. Down in the valleys it was nearly unbearable at times, especially for English folk who were unaccustomed to it. Both her pupils and staff wilted badly. Miss Holroyd made up her mind not to renew her lease but to try to find another house higher up on one of the mountain shelves, where things ought to be better.

She spent every spare moment of the second half of the term hunting, and just when she was about to give it up for another term or two, she was fortunate enough to hear of a small guest house in the Oberland which was closing down. She treated herself to a free weekend and went to investigate. She found the place would suit her in many ways. There was a meadow she could lease for games a little further along the shelf, and a mountain railway served the village.

The other three members of the staff who were most concerned agreed. It was decided that, when the school broke up, Miss Ashley should go home for a fortnight or three weeks—a fortnight, she said—while the other three saw to the removal of St Hilda's belongings. Then she would return and Miss Kent and Mrs Thwaites would depart for their holiday. The new term must begin ten days late, but that couldn't be helped. The parents made no particular objection in the circumstances. A busy time ensued.

The girls were to meet Miss Kent, the escort mistress, at Dover. Mrs Thwaites was to meet the Paris-Vienna express at Basle to help with the changes, and so it happened that on the last evening of the holidays Miss Holroyd and Miss Ashley were left to hold the fort.

"We begin with thirty-seven girls this term," the Head said as she stirred her after-dinner coffee thoughtfully. "As soon as we are really settled, I shall see about engaging another mistress for the Easter term. Someone for science. In the meantime I've contacted that big school further to the south of us—the Chalet School—and they're going to lend us one of their science people for two half-days every week for this term. They are really very pleasant and most helpful. Their girls will play ours at hockey and netball, so that's an advantage. In the summer there'll be tennis. I'm hoping, too, that later on we may be able to share in lectures and concerts. But, of course, that's all in the future."

"Let's hope they won't try to interfere with us and run us!" Miss Ashley said abruptly.

Miss Holroyd looked surprised. "My dear girl, why ever should they?"

"Well, from all I can hear, they're not only a big school but they've been out here for years. They may think that gives them the right to chip in, and I'd rather we stood on our own feet."

Miss Holroyd laughed. "What nonsense! From all I can hear, they are far too busy to think of that. They have all kinds of outside interests—plays, concerts, a garden fête in aid of the big Görnetz Platz Sanatorium each summer, and half-a-dozen other activities. And so far as I'm concerned, if they like to pass along any useful tips, I'll accept them gratefully. For pity's sake, don't take up that sort of attitude, Miriam!"

Miss Ashley was silenced, but she remained unconvinced. Miss Holroyd gave her a quick look and decided to leave things to time. She knew Miriam Ashley and she was aware that talking only made her more obstinate. At the same time, she meant to remain alert and if she saw that the girl was likely to make things difficult in any way, she would speak to some purpose. Bethia Holroyd was fond of Miriam, but St Hilda's must not suffer for her nonsense.

"We may expect the girls some time in the late afternoon," she said now, changing the subject. "The express reached Basle about seven in the morning. Mrs Thwaites will meet them and Miss Kent and take them to have a meal and brush-up. Then they catch a train for Interlaken and from there they get the ferry to the far end of Lake Brienz, and then it's not long in the mountain railway."

"They'll be half-dead, I expect," Miss Ashley responded. "It's a tiresome kind of journey with so many changes. That was one advantage about being at Geneva.

10

However, you can't have everything and really, the heat last term was enough to take the starch out of anyone. It'll be early bed for them, won't it, Miss Holroyd?"

"It certainly will," Miss Holroyd said emphatically. "And, considering what a busy day we shall have tomorrow, I think it had better be early bed for us tonight. If you'll take the coffee things to the kitchen, I'll just go the rounds and then we'll rest while we can."

They parted for the night and soon Miriam, at least, was fast asleep. Miss Holroyd, with much more at stake, was restless, dozing and waking by turns. Much later, she was to be thankful indeed for that. If she had slept as soundly as her young colleague, there would have been a tragedy and this story would not have been written.

It was after midnight when disaster came. Miss Holroyd had just got up to see if a beaker of hot milk would help her to sleep, when she stopped by her open window to sniff curiously. The next moment, she had slammed the window shut and was rushing down the corridor to Miss Ashley's room, shouting, "Fire—fire!" at the top of her voice.

Miriam Ashley took some rousing, but when she was out of bed, her clothes thrust into her arms by Miss Holroyd, and herself pushed into the corridor, she came to her senses with a rush. There could be no mistake. St Hilda's new home was alight. It was mainly of wood and, in the breeze that had sprung up with the turn of the night, it would be ablaze in less than no time. There was no chance to save anything much. Miss Holroyd rushed to her study to snatch her papers from her desk and hurl them out of the window into the courtyard beyond. Then she remembered the school cat, Minette, in the kitchen and dashed to the rescue.

By this time, the entire village was roused. While woodmen hurried to fight the flames away from the precious pines furring the mountain slopes, others trained

11

in firefighting rushed to do what they could for the new school. Luckily, the day before had been wet with heavy showers and that made the risk to the trees much less. But the school must go.

Miss Ashley staggered out into the air and looked round. "Miss Holroyd!" she shrieked. "Oh, she's gone after Minette!"

She turned to try to dash in again, but one of the men caught her and held her back. At the same moment, Minette came round the corner of the burning building, swelled to twice her normal size with terror. After her came a brawny mountaineer, carrying Miss Holroyd across his shoulders. She was quite unconscious and her night-clothes hung in tatters round her, but as they laid her down at a safe distance from the fire she moaned.

Miss Ashley knelt beside her, while one of the women brought a blanket and laid it over the injured woman.

News of the calamity spread like wildfire all over the area, including the Görnetz Platz. Dr Maynard, head of the Sanatorium there, had called on his forces and now they arrived with stretchers and bearers, medical supplies, nurses and doctors, headed by Dr Maynard himself.

Miss Ashley was scorched in several places, none of them serious, though they would be sore enough for the next few days, and her nerves were strained with the shock. Miss Holroyd had come off much worse. A falling beam had broken her ankle and all her left side was scorched severely. An injection ended pain for the time being and the medical party did what they could on the spot. Then she was laid on a stretcher and borne off down the mountain slope to the road where an ambulance was waiting. Miss Ashley had been whisked off to it before that, and given a dose of something to calm her until they could get her to bed. Miss Wilson, Head of St Mildred's, the finishing branch of the Chalet School, had come with the party and she insisted that the mistress should be taken to the school.

"She's not badly hurt," she said. "She'll want to be near their own girls and of course they must come to us, for the moment anyhow. You can drop us at the school on your way and Matey and our own nurse will see to her. Don't argue, Jack! There's nothing else to do."

So it was that when Miriam Ashley finally roused up early in the following afternoon, she found herself in bed in a white cubicle she had never seen before, while a strange nurse was standing at the bedside, smiling at her.

"What's happened?" Miss Ashley demanded when she was fully awake. Then: "Oh! The fire! Miss Holroyd! She's all right, isn't she? Is this a hospital? Can I go and see her? Oh, she's all right, surely?"

The nurse nodded. "She's at the Sanatorium and you're here at the Chalet School, so I'm afraid you can't go and see her this minute. But you needn't worry. She's being well looked after. You'll hear all about that presently. Meanwhile, here comes a meal for you. You ought to be hungry after such a lengthy sleep." She raised her voice. "Herein, Trüdchen!"

A girl entered with a tray while the nurse piled up pillows at her patient's back, set a folding bed-table over her knees and finally put the tray on it.

"Now," she said cheerily, "let's see what you can do with this and then you shall hear all the news."

"Oh, but I must know what's happened!" Miriam Ashley said. "What time is it? What's happening to the school? When can I go to see the Head? Someone must take hold and it'll have to be me—"

"Now that's enough," Nurse interrupted. "Not another word until you've emptied that bowl and plate. Then you shall hear everything."

And she had to be obeyed. For once, Miss Ashley had met with someone who paid no heed to her protests, and she had to drink every drop of the delicious soup and eat the bread twist that accompanied it before she heard any more news.

Even then, she had a feeling that she wasn't told half. She heard that Miss Holroyd had broken an ankle and sustained one or two nasty burns. She was being kept under drugs for the present and was as well as could be expected. Nurse would bring a later bulletin in the evening. As for the school, it was to come to the Chalet School until they could see what arrangements could be made. Word had been sent to Basle to Mrs Thwaites and Miss Kent and they would all come up to the Görnetz Platz in the Chalet School coaches.

"So you needn't worry about them for the next few days," wound up Miss Wilson who had brought the news. "Your best plan is to keep quiet, sleep all you can; take all Nurse gives you and in a few days you'll be yourself again and able to cope. At present, you can't and no one is going to let you try."

"But I must go and see Miss Holroyd and find out what she wants done," Miss Ashley protested.

"Not for the next few days you can't," Miss Wilson told her firmly. She glanced over her shoulder at Nurse who came forward, syringe in hand. "Now Nurse is going to give you a little shot to ease the pain of your burns and help you to sleep. When you wake up after that, you'll feel much better and more able to cope. All right, Nurse." She nodded and left the room.

Later on, when Nurse came to the drawing room where Miss Wilson, her co-Head, Miss Annersley, and Matey, as everyone at the Chalet School called the Senior Matron, were drinking coffee, she spoke her mind clearly.

"Talk of obstinate! It's her middle name! We'll have our own troubles with her, once she's better. However, she's well over and likely to stay so till tomorrow morning. But my goodness, she's going to take some handling!"

"Oh, she'll realise when she rouses tomorrow that she can't do much but lie still for a day or two," Miss Annersley said soothingly. "You must make allowance for

14

shock, Nurse. Jack Maynard says she's far more badly shocked than she knows. As for Miss Holroyd, poor soul, she can have no visitors for many a long day to come."

"What's the latest?" Nurse asked anxiously.

"No change. It's too soon to be able to say what may happen. They can only wait. But what a way to begin a new term!"

"Yes," Miss Wilson agreed. "We do get 'em, don't we?" Then with a chuckle she added, "Jo's going to eat her finger-ends at being out of all this. Serves her right for being in such a tearing hurry to see the new Embury baby, girl or not!"

Chapter 2

SHOCK FOR ST HILDA'S

GILLIE GARSTIN was the first of the St Hilda girls to wake up next morning. She sat up in her little bed and gazed round the pretty curtains with their scatter of globe flowers, gold on cream, and then glanced up at the casement window at the right-hand side of her bed. It was all frightfully nice and a jolly sight better idea to have cubicles instead of just beds in a row. Yes; she liked it—for a change, anyhow.

Having settled so much, Gillie turned to events. Whoever would have thought so much could happen in such a short time? First they had been met at Victoria station by Miss Kent: but that was what usually happened. In fact, now she came to think of it, everything had been usual until they reached Basle. Then Gillie remembered the girls they had seen drawn up in long files on the platform of the Gare du Nord and obviously waiting for the same train as themselves. That was where it all began!

The thing which had first caught the eye was their uniform. Such a lovely, deep blue! And when one girl had turned round to speak to someone behind her, her open coat had swung to show that she was wearing a proper dress—not a gym tunic. The St Hilda girls had thought it was just a Sunday frock, but now it seemed that it was the school uniform. And was it the tops, with its honeycombing in crimson at waist and shoulders and the little white revers at the neck!

Not that Miss Kent had given her charges much time to stare. She had been too anxious to get them safely into the train with all their cases and umbrellas and the rest of their belongings. She had counted them over three times!

The journey itself had been without incident until they reached Basle, where they had to leave the great Vienna express and catch another to Interlaken. Miss Kent had told them the details of their journey to the Hellerdorf where the home of the new school was.

"Only it didn't turn out as planned," Gillie remembered. "We saw the Chalet School hopping out and we hopped out, too, and then that Mlle of theirs came racing up to that big, pretty mistress who was in charge and Matron came haring over to us and then it all began!"

Miss Kent and Matron had joined up and Mlle and her friend had joined them and they had all gone at it, hot and strong. Miss Kent had exclaimed in horrified tones, though the girls were too far away to hear what was being said. The next thing, Matron had come over to them, called them to order and told them the awful news that their new school had been burned to the ground overnight and Miss Holroyd and Miss Ashley had both been injured, Miss Holroyd quite badly. Before St Hilda's had fully grasped that, Matron had gone on to say that the Chalet School on the Görnetz Platz had come forward to offer them shelter for the present until something could be arranged for them. The school had gone with all its furniture and books and everything else. Their trunks had most mercifully been held up in Interlaken and would be sent up as soon as possible to the Görnetz Platz. But otherwise, they had no school and nothing to go to.

"However," Matron went on before anyone could do more than exclaim with horror, "we are not homeless, thanks to the Chalet School who are taking us in for the present. They have their own coaches which are waiting outside in the Bahnhof Platz and you are to follow them. They will squeeze us in somehow, Miss Wilmot says." She added, "I know I needn't warn you to behave yourselves well. We are all terribly anxious about Miss Holroyd and all this has come on us as a shock."

17

That long coach run had been fun in one way, even if they had been crowded. One thing Gillie and her friends had noticed was that they seemed to have girls from several different countries at the Chalet School. They heard French and German being spoken on all sides, as well as two or three other languages which, at the moment, they didn't identify. There were ten of Class Middles B at St Hilda's—the lowest form of all—and four of them had been squeezed in with a whole bunch of Chaletians of their own age. Gillie had seen to it that the three who went with her were her own gang. Besides them, there were a number of big girls who sat at the back of the coach. When the chatter among their juniors became too noisy, one of them checked it pleasantly, but quite firmly, and her command was obeyed instantly.

"Bossers, aren't they?" Anne Crozier had muttered to Gillie as they sat together.

"They'll need to be with crowds like this," Gillie replied. "Besides, those girls are older than ours, some of them—quite grown-up they look."

Kitty Anderson, sitting in front, turned round. "How many do you think there are?" she muttered.

"Goodness! How should I know?" Gillie demanded. "Hundreds, I should think."

She raised her voice incautiously and the girl sitting nearest her on the other side of the aisle leaned across to say with a smile, "Only around four hundred. I say, you don't belong to us. Well, you've a different uniform for one thing. Why are you joining up? Is a new school starting on the Platz? What a lark if it is!"

Barbara Hewlett meant to be friendly but, to the four who already felt rather out of things, her tone seemed very superior and they ruffled up at once like young turkeycocks.

"We're St Hilda's School," Gillie told her curtly.

"Oh? One of our Houses is dedicated to St Hild. I

suppose that's the same one," Barbara said, while the two girls crushed into the same seat with her, bent forward to look. "Why are you coming with us, though?"

"Our school's been burnt down," Anne explained. "We've nowhere to go and your Head has offered to take us. In fact," she added with a giggle, "we're refugees!"

"How ghastly!" exclaimed Barbara. "I say! That's a bit of a bind, isn't it?"

"Still, we ought to be able to tuck them all in," one of her friends put in. "After all, don't forget we have a new House this term. There aren't an awful lot of you, are there?"

"Thirty-something," Kitty said. "What're your names? We can't go on just saying 'you' all the time. It's a bit sniffy, isn't it? I'm Kitty Anderson and these other three are Anne Crozier, Mary Candlish and Gillie Garstin."

Gillie had got so far in her pondering, when suddenly a big bell boomed out, startling her into a violent jump. It was followed by a series of groans and then a very sweet, clear voice called, "Show a leg! Show a leg!"

There came a series of thuds and Gillie, guessing that everyone was getting up, followed suit and stood on her rug, wondering what she must do next. She soon learned, for her curtains were parted and a tall girl, whose curly chestnut hair tumbled in two thick pigtails down to her waist, looked in with a smile.

"A new girl?" she said. "Tell me your name, my lamb. Someone seems to have slipped up, for there isn't any name on your curtains."

"I'm not—not new, I mean," Gillie explained. "Actually, I don't belong."

"Oh, one of the St Hilda girls! I see! The Head told us about the affair last night, of course. Welcome to the Chalet School, anyhow. And now, what is your name?"

"Gillie Garstin."

"Thank you. Well, Gillie, when you hear me call 'Show

a leg!' you do just that. Run to your curtains and shove a leg out. Then I know you're up. I'm Len Maynard, by the way, dormitory prefect here." She paused. Then she called, "Jack Lambert!"

There was a scuffle and a girl of Gillie's age appeared. Gillie had seen her on the coach the day before, but at the far end. At supper, she had also been at the opposite end of the table and as everyone up to Lower IVa had been packed off to bed as soon as Prayers were over, they had no chance to meet.

"This is Gillie Garstin of St Hilda's, Jack," Len said. "Do sheepdog for her, will you?"

"Yes, Len," Jack replied; and Len nodded and moved on down the aisle.

Jack—never was a girl better named!—gave Gillie a grin and remarked, "Come on, and we'll find out which bather you're in and when." And she marched Gillie to the door on which hung a board. Jack scanned the timetable fastened to it and nodded. "OK. You're fourth bath in 1C. That means you have last bath. You'd better strip your bed and say your prayers while you're waiting. You come after Renata van Buren. I'll give you a yell when she comes back and take you along. You can have your bath either cold or lukewarm, and for pity's sake mind you leave the bather tidy and unsplashed or Matron will have something to say. I'm second in B, and here's Mollie Rossiter coming back so I must scram. You go back and do as I said. I'll come to you when I get back."

Jack shot off to rescue her towels and Gillie was left to return to her cubicle, kneel down to say her prayers, and then to drag off her bedclothes and toss them over her chair. By that time, Jack had returned and must have torn through bath and dressing, for she arrived to take Gillie to her bath fully dressed, with even her cropped black hair smooth and shining.

"Here you are," she announced, ushering the stranger

into a bathing cubicle. "Better hurry. There isn't a lot of time left. Renata always takes an age." Then she departed, and Gillie obeyed her and made such speed with her bath that she only partly dried herself and had to finish off in her cubicle before she dressed.

Jack arrived while she was knotting her tie and instantly set to work on her mattress. "Hump it up every morning," she explained as Gillie stared at her. "Every other morning, you turn it, of course. Always shove your pillow over the window sill unless the weather's unspeakable. Hang up your pyjamas on those hooks to air—I'll do it now—and shove your slippers on the rack. There! That's done! Your dressing gown on this hook. Now are you ready? There's the bell—come on!"

Feeling breathless with the speed she had made, Gillie followed her guide down the narrow aisle at the back of the dormitory to join on to the line of girls already formed up there, with Len watching them. As the dormitory immediately next to them marched out, Gillie saw Kitty and Anne, both looking as dazed as she felt. Then Len gave the order to march and they went off down the corridor, down the stairs, along two passages and finally found themselves in a big sunny room with windows on two sides, bookcases piled with books running halfway up the walls, and a number of chairs, small tables and a couple of long settees for furniture. Prints of famous pictures hung on the walls and the window sills bore flowering plants and vases at present filled with michaelmas daisies.

"Our common room," Jack explained. "We'll see plenty of it later on when the bad weather comes. Just at present, we'll be out every minute we can."

"Why?" Gillie asked.

"Because bad weather, especially up here, often means staying in for days on end. 'Scuse me, please. Barbara wants me." And Jack sped across the room, leaving Gillie alone.

Kitty and Anne had been watching and they rushed to her at once.

"Oh, Gillie, how did you get on?" Kitty asked eagerly. "What's your dormitory called? We two are in Anemone. It's awfully pretty—cream curtains with red and purple anemones all over them and bedside rugs to match and so are the counterpanes. But oh, Gillie, the prefect is a French girl and she spoke to us in French at first. I did feel ghastly!"

"But when she saw we didn't understand, she spoke in English," Anne chimed in. "Quite decent English, too. Meg Walton—that's her over there; that girl with the red pigtail—says they can all speak three languages—more or less. They have to. I say, you don't think they'll make us try to do it while we're here, do you? I can read a bit of French, but I can't say much more than 'Bonjour' or 'Merci beaucoup'. As for German, I don't know the first thing about it. For goodness' sake, tell us what you think!"

"I haven't a clue. Oh, I shouldn't think so," Gillie said optimistically.

The rest of their form joined up with them at this point, and a moment later a gong sounded and at once everyone in the room rushed to line up by the door. Jack and some other girls came to take charge of those girls whom they had been told to "sheepdog", as the Chalet School called it, and Gillie found herself pushed between Jack and the red-headed Meg Walton, while Anne was next to Meg and after her came another Chalet School girl and then Kitty. When they had settled down at the breakfast table, the St Hilda girls found that they had been nicely distributed all round in this way. Nor were they the only ones. There were quite a number of new girls as well, and Gillie noticed that they were looked after very thoroughly.

Breakfast—only they called it "Frühstück" here—was rather a shock to the St Hilda people. Miss Holroyd had kept to British meals as far as she could, and a breakfast consisting of huge cups of milky coffee, rolls and butter, jam and fruit, did not strike the hungry Gillie and her chums as ideal. They said nothing, of course, but Gillie, looking up, caught the eye of Mary Candlish, seated opposite her, and knew that they were thinking alike.

After Frühstück, they had to go upstairs to make their beds and tidy their cubicles. Then down again to what they learned were called "Splasheries" here, to change into walking-shoes and pull on coats and berets, and then out for a brisk walk in the morning sunshine and air that seemed to fill you with tremendous vigour. Talking was permitted and the St Hilda folk were rather appalled to hear every girl speaking in English, French or German as she chose. Jack, partnering Gillie, explained that until Monday they might speak any one of the three. After that they must use the language for the day.

"But what happens when you don't know the first word of it?" Gillie asked.

Jack grinned. "You soon learn. Everyone goes on at you till you do. And you know, Gillie," she went on, "when you hear a language all round you and nothing else but, you do pick up things in no time—unless you're stupid, of course."

"Oh?" Gillie said politely. But she made up her mind then and there that if they must conform to Chalet School rules while they were there, she for one wasn't going to have people thinking she was slow-witted. If it killed her, she would do her best to speak French or German, even if she had to spend some of her free time learning lists and lists of words and verbs and genders!

When they got back to the school, they had to change again into house shoes. Luckily, the St Hilda girls had had theirs in their cases, so that was no difficulty. Then they went back to the common room, but only for about five minutes. The bell rang and they lined up, and while Catholics went to the gym for Prayers with the Catholic mistresses, all the rest, including St Hilda's marched to the Hall. Here, at long last, the smaller school found themselves located in a bunch at one side, with Miss Kent and Matron beside them. Miss Kent explained that later on they would be assigned to various forms. At present they were to stay together.

"But Miss Annersley will explain it to you presently," she finished.

"Miss Kent, how is Miss Holroyd?" Mary Murrell, Head Prefect of St Hilda's, asked anxiously.

"No change yet," Miss Kent said. "And I'm afraid it'll be that way for the next few days. But Miss Ashley is going on well, though she's poorly and feverish today," she added. "However, I expect that by Monday she will be well enough to come into school. And in the meantime, the Chalet School staff will help us out. We have a great deal to be thankful for."

The second bell rang then, so no more could be said. Prayers followed, and after Prayers everyone sat down. The Catholics marched in and took their places and then Miss Annersley rose from the big chair in which she had been sitting, came to lean on the lectern and began to speak.

Chapter 3

NEW ARRANGEMENTS

FOUR hundred and odd pairs of eyes, most of them wide with curiosity and excitement, fixed themselves on Miss Annersley's face. Even the Chalet girls felt it. Never, so far as the present generation was concerned, had there been such a sensational beginning of term. It had been exciting enough before, with a new House added to the school and new, extra mistresses, not to speak of having the Kindergarten included in the school. With another school, however small, added to their numbers, they were all agog. How would things be arranged? Would this other school come in with them or have form rooms of its own and work apart? What would they do about prefects? Even the Chalet School's own prefects were anxious to know this.

Miss Annersley, standing at the lectern, smiling down at them, knew all about it, of course. There was not much she did not know about the girls. But before she could relieve their curiosity on such minor matters, she had other things to say first.

"First," she said, her beautiful voice reaching easily to the far end of Hall, though she certainly didn't seem to raise it, "I know the St Hilda girls will be anxious to have the very latest news of Miss Holroyd. There is no change at present in her condition. She is very ill from shock as well as her burns and broken ankle. For the next two or three days, no one can say how things are likely to go. She is quite unconscious and until she rouses up, there is very little to be done. There is one thing all of you—and I speak to the Chalet School as well as to St Hilda's—can do. Pray for her."

She paused there and some of the younger St Hilda's

girls stared at each other, rather startled. This was something they had not thought of. But she went on and they had to listen.

"I have better news of Miss Ashley. She, mercifully, was only scorched comparatively lightly. She is poorly and feverish today, but the doctors are not anxious about her. They say she will soon pick up, once she has got over the shock. A few days of quiet and rest in our own sanatorium will see to that. Probably she will be able to take up her work again by the end of next week. But you must all remember that she has had a horrible experience and will feel its effects for the next few weeks.

"Now as to yourselves. We are very full up this term —too full to be able to allot separate form rooms to St Hilda's, as Miss Ashley told me she had hoped. The only thing we can do is to fit you in among our own girls as far as possible. We've done that already with the dormitories, as you know. I hope we can manage it with the form rooms. We are leaving you St Hilda girls in your own forms and placing those with girls of the same age; but that is only for the moment. As soon as we have some idea about your standards of work, we may find that we have to move some of you to other forms. That won't mean that some of you are stupid and some bright. It will simply mean that we feel you can do better work in some other form. Miss Holroyd once explained to me that, owing to shortage of staff, she had to put girls together who really either could not or ought not to be doing the same work, and she hoped that this state of things would end as soon as possible. Here, we have a number of forms so there won't be the same difficulty. As for how long you are likely to be with us, that must depend on Miss Holroyd's recovery. We all hope you will be very happy and enjoy your sojourn, even if it isn't your own school. You must keep together and be loyal to St Hilda's and your own Head. At the same time, as long as you are with us, I'm

26

afraid you must conform to certain of our rules—the languages question, for instance." She paused there and stood looking down at them with dancing eyes that picked up one lugubrious face after another, especially among the younger St Hilda girls.

"Oh, of course you must fall in with that rule," she said briskly. "It would be simply impossible to make any exceptions. You won't find it so difficult after the beginning —and now I'm speaking to everyone who has come for the first time this term. Until Monday, you may use any language you like. On Monday, school rules are in full force for everyone, though for the first fortnight, newcomers are excused a little so long as they really try to speak other languages than their own on the appropriate days. After that, you come under the same system as everyone else—a centime fine every time you break the rule."

"Oh gosh!" Anne Crozier groaned. "How much pocket-money shall we have left at that rate?"

She stopped suddenly, for Meg Walton was nudging her fiercely.

"Now about prefects," Miss Annersley was going on serenely. "I know you have them. Who is head of them, please?"

There was a little awkward pause. Then Mary Murrell stood up, touching her spectacles nervously. "I am, Miss Annersley—Mary Murrell. We haven't voted for the others yet, but I expect they will include Monica Garstin at any rate."

"Thank you, Mary," the Head said with a friendly smile. "We must make arrangements for the voting as soon as we can. Then those girls who are chosen will join our own prefects. Maeve," she glanced at the Chalet School's own Head Girl, "will you see to all that for me, please. As soon as we know who the St Hilda prefects are, you had better call a meeting and arrange about duties and so on. But I'll see you in the study presently."

27

Maeve, a tall, athletic-looking girl with a pleasant face and manner, stood up to say "Yes, Miss Annersley." Then she cast a matey grin at Mary Murrell before she sat down again.

"Then that is all we can do about St Hilda's for the moment," the Head said.

"And quite enough, too," muttered Marian Hadaway, a fifteen-year-old of St Hilda's, who was given to finding fault with most school arrangements.

"Dry up!" Katherine Rutherford, seated next to her, advised.

Miss Annersley was reading out the list of those who had passed various exams, and some of the elder St Hilda girls were slightly stunned at the number and the very high standard some of them seemed to have attained. Everyone who had been entered had passed GCE and most of them had a credit or two as well. Two girls who had left had won scholarships in music and the school applauded loudly. But they made even more noise over the news that two girls had won cups in tennis tournaments, slightly to the relief of Gillie and her chums, who had been feeling appalled at the long exam lists.

"I've one thing to say that some of you won't like," the Head said, smiling broadly. "As we have begun term so late, half term must be cut to the minimum. Work will go on till the end of the Friday morning and you must all understand that there will be no going away this term. We are trying to arrange expeditions for you for the Saturday and Monday. School will start again on the Tuesday. Yes; I know it's a big change, but remember you have had almost a fortnight more holiday than usual this summer. That has to be made up as far as possible. I may add," she went on, "that the staff are preparing something very special for the Saturday evening, though I don't know what it is yet.

"Finally, there is our nativity play at the end of term. Mrs Maynard is writing it for us as Lady Russell is in

Australia—at least, they sail next week. While she is away, she will try to find some curiosities for the Sarah Denny Museum. Also, whoever is editor of *The Chaletian* this year, Josette and Sybil have promised accounts of the voyage and their adventures in Australia for our magazine.

"Now I think that is all for the moment. Miss Dene will read out the form lists. As soon as a list is finished, will the girls in that form please march quietly to their form room—all, that is, except the two Sixths who will go straight to Matron for unpacking."

The Head sat down, signing to her secretary to read out the form lists, and a fair, pretty woman in the thirties stood up and read off the names, pausing between each form long enough to give the girls time to leave the Hall. As each form marched out, its form mistress followed, and presently there were left in Hall only the Head, Miss Dene, the mistress at the piano, the St Hilda girls and Miss Kent. The girls looked anxiously to Miss Annersley. They were all longing to know what their fate was going to be. Miss Kent looked hardly less anxious. She knew there had been far too little time for anything definite to be settled.

Miss Annersley left the dais and came quickly to the rather forlorn little group. She gave them a warm smile before she spoke.

"Don't look so upset, girls," she said. "We can't give you definite places yet, but for the present we are putting you, as I told you, with girls of more or less your own ages. Mary Murrell, I should like your form and the next to go to your dormitories for unpacking. Maeve and the other prefects will look after you."

"Thank you, Miss Annersley," Mary said. She glanced round at the eight other people who made up the two forms and they followed her at once.

Miss Annersley turned to the others. "Get into lines

with the next form leading and the others following—in your old forms," she said. "I'll take you along to the form rooms and introduce you myself. Come along, girls! Miss Dene, I'll see you in the office in twenty minutes' time. We have a good deal to see to this morning."

Then she shepherded her new lambs out of Hall, and their new school careers began in less than ten minutes.

Chapter 4

Minette Sets The Ball Rolling

It was Saturday morning. Home letters had been written
and any oddments of preparation left over from the
previous night were finished. Elevenses had been taken
early and now everyone was outside enjoying the
September sunshine and fresh breeze—everyone, that is
to say, except the three lower forms of St Hilda's, who
were doing test papers so that they might be properly
placed in the school and begin fair on the Monday.

This made it possible for the Chalet girls to voice their
opinions on the latest event among themselves. The two
senior forms of St Hilda's were already on the hockey
field—with the exception of Monica Garstin, Mary
Murrell and Hilda Matthieson from the form below them,
who had all exclaimed that they would like to try lacrosse
and were hard at work with a number of other learners,
being firmly coached by Ruey Richardson, captain of
lacrosse.

The Lower Fourths played netball. They were standing
about on the pitches, waiting until Monica Caird, the
games prefect, could come and tell them what to do.
Lower IVa were eagerly practising passing and shooting
on one pitch, and some of the B division were following
suit. The rest stood in a huddle talking, with Jack Lambert
in the middle.

"Well, chaps, what do you think about it all?" she
demanded, keeping a wary eye on the path for any sign of
Monica or others of the school's grandees.

"I do not like it," Renata van Buren said, with a toss of
her flaxen pigtails. "I do not like having so many in form
and I do not like these girls. This is our school and they

31

are trying to get the best seats and books for themselves. They are only visitors and they ought to wait until we tell them what they may do."

Jack's black eyes sparkled and she grinned. "You only say that because that girl Susan what's-her-name tried to bag the seat you wanted."

"Be careful! Here is Monica," Wanda von Eschenau warned them as the tall girl came striding across from the third hockey pitch to start them off on netball practice.

The chatter ceased at once. Monica was an excellent games prefect, a good coach and ready to give all she had to people who really tried. But she did insist on full attention. If she did not get it, she spoke her mind freely to the culprits and her tongue had quite a nasty edge to it on such occasions.

Now, she quickly set various people to picking up for teams, and when that was done she sent two sets of fourteen over to the pitches where Rosamund Lilley and a friend of hers, Len Maynard, were waiting to start them off. Another set went to the next pitch—the school had six altogether—in charge of Betty Landon; and a fourth she started herself, leaving Jack Lambert's and Wanda von Eschenau's two teams and the few who had not been picked to await her pleasure. What the two teams ought to have done was to take their places in readiness, but at that moment Minette, the complacent tabby cause of Miss Holroyd's serious illness, came strolling across the pitch. Minette had settled down comfortably in the Chalet kitchen. When she felt so disposed, she made excursions to other parts of the school. She was accustomed to girls and was a friendly cat and now she came to rub up against Jack Lambert's ankles, purring loudly.

"Isn't she a pet?" Meg Walton exclaimed, lifting her and tickling her chin.

"She does keep herself clean, doesn't she?" observed Margaret Twiss. "Just look at her spotless paws!"

32

It was at this point that Monica, having started off the teams headed by Arda Peik and Barbara Hewlett, arrived to find her last sets in a huddle round Minette instead of waiting eagerly in their places. She was righteously indignant and sent them to their posts with a good deal of asperity.

"Jack and Wanda! What are you thinking about? Get your teams into order at once! Put the cat down, Meg! You are here for netball; not for playing with a cat! Shoo! Scat! Scram, you nuisance!"

Meg dropped Minette as if she were red hot and fled to take up her position as goal defence, while the indignant Minette stalked to the edge of the pitch and sat down, glaring at them.

"And that's not safe, either!" Monica continued. "Some of you will be trampling on her! Here, Jack Lambert! You're a decent runner. Pick her up and take her to Karen in the kitchen and don't dilly-dally, either! I'll give you five minutes there and back. Hurry!"

Jack swooped down on Minette and sped off, arriving at the corner of the main building just as Gillie Garstin, Mary Candlish and Kitty Anderson, who had finished a hair-raising arithmetic paper and had ten minutes before their next test, came round from the other direction, having been sent out to stretch their legs and get a breath of fresh air.

"What on earth are you doing with our cat?" Mary asked sharply.

Jack gave her a grin. "She came to watch the netball prac, but Monica didn't see it in the same light and told me to take her to Karen pronto."

"Here, give her to me!" Mary snatched at Minette and tried to haul her away. Minette had stuck her claws firmly into Jack's sweater and clung for all she was worth. She was not frightened, but she was vexed at being shooed and then picked up and rushed away like that. Mary's grabbing put the finishing touch to her rage. She swelled, spat, and scratched Mary with one paw while she still clung with the other three.

"Don't clutch her like that, you idiot!" Jack exclaimed crossly. "You're frightening her! Hi, Minette! Don't claw me like that! You'll have my new sweater in rags! Gently, old lady!"

Mary flushed. "She's our cat! You've no right to lug her about like that!"

"I wasn't. Monica told me to take her," Jack said, contriving to get the last claw free and setting Minette on the ground. "There you are! Take her! I don't want her! Just look what she's done to my sweater!"

"Poor Minette!" Gillie said, stooping to pick her up. But Minette had had enough. With a final outburst of shocking language, she dabbed at Gillie before turning and fleeing into the shrubbery.

"You'd better go to Matron with that scratch," Jack advised Mary as she turned to race back at top speed. Monica was annoyed already and she dared not delay.

Mary and Kitty were already pelting after Minette who had retired under some bushes and was lying low and refusing to come out. She declined flatly to be drawn and when Miss Ferrars, having waited an extra five minutes for them, came to find out what they were doing, all three were flat on their stomachs, regardless of dirt and dead leaves, still coaxing her. The mistress gave them short shrift. She ordered them up pretty sharply and sent them to tidy themselves with a comment that made their ears burn. Only Mary had temerity enough to murmur something about Minette.

"Don't trouble about the cat," Miss Ferrars rejoined severely. "She can look after herself well enough. What matters is that you ought to have been doing dictation seven minutes ago and you've wasted all that time for yourselves, the other girls and me! Now hurry up and make yourselves fit to be seen, and don't behave in that babyish way again, please." With which she turned on her heel and stalked off to her own form room, where the tests were being taken.

Naturally, the three were furious at being spoken to in that way. They were too young to understand that the beginning of term was a crowded time for all members of staff; that Miss Ferrars had voluntarily broken into her own free time to relieve someone else who was even busier than she; and that in so large a school, reins had to be drawn tighter than in a small one like St Hilda's. All the same, in those few minutes, Miss Ferrars pushed the ball on a little further and earned their deep dislike for most of the term.

Dictation was followed by French dictée in which the perturbed three did shockingly, Gillie even managing to misspell such words as "Vous avez" and "peut-être", which she knew perfectly well. Mercifully, dictée brought the tests to a close, but by the time it was over, the three had worked themselves up into a fine state of resentment and could scarcely speak civilly to anyone.

Mary in particular, who adored Minette, was raging. Not that she had any need to worry. Minette came strolling in when it suited her and settled down to a good dinner before visiting Miss Annersley's pretty salon where she had already learned that a small saucer of cream might be forthcoming at that hour.

In the afternoon, the girls went for rambles, each form going separately. The Juniors and Middles had mistresses as escorts; but the three Fifths were allowed to go in charge of prefects and the rest of the two Sixths were sent off by themselves. They had their bounds and knew the few rules that governed rambles, and, as Miss Dene had once observed, if they couldn't be trusted at seventeen and eighteen to behave themselves, they never could be.

Lower IVa had their own form mistress, Miss Charlesworth, for escort. Miss Ferrars offered to go with her, an offer gratefully accepted. Miss Charlesworth had some of the worst imps in the school among her form. Furthermore, now that the form had swollen to thirty-five girls, she felt it would be just as well if there were two people to keep an eye on them.

"We're going down to Lauterbach," she said when she joined the double line waiting on the side path. "Have you all got partners? Then listen a moment. You must croc until we turn down beyond the railway. After that you may break ranks and go in groups of not less than four or more than six. People in front must remember not to go too far ahead. Miss Ferrars and I will see to the laggards." She ended with a laugh in which all the Chalet girls joined. St Hilda's, having by this time heard the story of Minette's doings and Miss Ferrars' callousness over the cat, remained stolidly serious and silent. Gillie and Co. were by way of being leaders among their kind and the tale, as told by them, lost nothing.

Miss Ferrars glanced at the grim-looking ten with a little surprise but said nothing. Miss Charlesworth sent her most responsible pair, Barbara Hewlett and Mollie Rossiter, to head the procession and they set off.

Needless to state, St Hilda girls were paired with St Hilda girls. Jack had invited Gillie Garstin to be her partner and had been snubbed by a stately, "Thank you; but I already have a partner." After that, the Chalet girls left the newcomers to "stew in their own juice" as Barbara succinctly put it. Further, since they knew nothing about the district, Miss Charlesworth had placed the St Hilda girls in a solid block in the middle of the crocodile. She didn't want to have to waste time hunting for people who had strayed away and lost themselves.

"Though how you imagine they could do it on that path," Miss Ferrars said, "is more than I can understand. There's the embankment on the railway side and on the other it's mostly well above their head."

"Quite climbable, though," Miss Charlesworth pointed out, "and there are those two turnings halfway down. By the way, Kathy, do you know where they lead? I've never investigated, though I've wondered more than once."

"Oh, just round the mountain to little shelves where some folk keep goats and sheep. I see your point about the girls, though. Better warn them not to try dodging along those paths when we break. Some of our own imps are quite capable of it."

When they did break, Gillie and Co. having recovered their tempers more or less in the fresh air, proceeded to enlarge on the morning's happenings. It was awkward that they might not go in groups of more than six, but they managed. Gillie and Mary expanded their story with much acerbity and when Kitty Anderson, who was slightly more level-headed in some ways than the other two, ventured to point out that Jack had said that Monica had told her to take Minette to the kitchen, she was vigorously suppressed by the other two.

"Don't be so stupid!" Gillie fumed. "You know that between them they upset Minette so that she clawed Mary good and hard and tried to claw me, too. That's not like Minette, poor pet! She's the sweetest-tempered cat that ever walked. Goodness knows how they treated her on the netball pitch. They must have frightened the wits out of her for her to behave like that!"

Mary chimed in. "Yes; and did we get into a row with Miss Ferrars for not being dead on time for her beastly dictation! She wouldn't hear of us trying to coax Minette out. The poor darling might have gone off somewhere and we might have lost her."

"Oh, how rotten of her!" Moira Baker cried. "Poor little Minette! Why, she might easily have lost herself—perhaps died of starvation on the mountain! I do call that a filthy thing to do!"

"But," put in Helen Henderson, "Minette was all right. I mean, she didn't go off. I saw her myself, crossing the entrance hall when we were taking our chairs to Hall for

37

the afternoon rest. Besides, she's never been kept in since we came. If she'd been going to run away, wouldn't she have done it sooner?"

"Well, it's no thanks to Jack Lambert that she didn't!" Mary snapped. "And anyhow, what right have those Chalet girls to interfere with our cat?"

"Well, if that Monica girl told her to take Minette to the kitchen she couldn't help herself, could she?" Helen asked reasonably. "They do seem to make such an awful lot of the prefects here."

"It's all poppycock!" Anne Crozier returned. "Oh, I know we more or less do what our own prefects tell us, but here, they literally run when one just lifts a finger." She turned to Gillie with a giggle. "How'll your own Monica enjoy that sort of thing? I should think it'll be a bit of a shock to her and Mary Murrell and the rest if we start in doing it here."

"Wonder how long we'll be stuck here?" Moira said.

"Let's hope not long," Mary growled. "I don't want to be here. I want us to be on our own and in our own school. It's sickening being part of another."

"It'll be till half term, anyhow," Gillie said positively. "Don't you remember what Miss Annersley said at Prayers—that Miss Holroyd's still very ill, though her heart was a little stronger and she had passed a better night, so the doctors were really hopeful of her? Well, if she's still as ill as all that, you bet she won't be fit to think of where to shove us before half term. In fact, I don't suppose she'll do it before next term."

"Oh, well, I expect Ashey will see to it," Kitty said comfortably. "She's the next boss, isn't she? And didn't someone say she was getting up today and would probably be in school in another week's time?"

"That's so," Helen agreed. "All the same, Kitty, the school isn't hers. It's Miss Holroyd who has the say-so. Oh, dear! What a muddle it all is!"

"Well, there's one thing," Gillie said. "Just you all remember that we belong to St Hilda's—not the Chalet School. We've got to stick together or they'll be trying to boss us out of existence."

"But we've got to be with them for lessons and all that," Helen reminded her.

"I didn't mean that. You are a dope, Helen! I meant out of school hours, we stick together and don't bother with them any more than we must. Now have you got it?"

Helen reddened. "You needn't be so rude about it, Gillie. Of course we'll all stick together."

"Oh, well, I didn't really mean anything," Gillie apologised. "Only what with Minette and the awful rowing we got from Miss Ferrars and everything else, you get mixed up."

Then they discovered that, in their absorption, they had dropped behind until they were nearly on top of the two mistresses and had to hurry on to get out of earshot so that they might talk as they chose.

Chapter 5

UNTER DEN KIEFERN

BARBARA looked round at the St Hilda girls and waved her hand impressively towards the big chalet which they had just reached. "This," she said, is Unter den Kiefern, where the Chalet School started in the Oberland. Really, it was St Mildred's only, but that was for just three terms. Then we all came out and began properly on the Görnetz Platz."

"But that is not quite true," Renata put in. "We were not at school then. It was seven years ago, and the youngest girls were people like Mary-Lou Trelawney and Vi Lucy and Hilary Bennet and all those girls. And now," she added sorrowfully, "even they have left St Mildred's and gone to universities and hospitals and places like that to train for their jobs."

"When did St Mildred's come up to the Görnetz Platz?" Mary Candlish asked.

"Oh, not for years—well, I think it's four years ago," Barbara said. "Yes; it must be 'cos I've been at the school for three years now and it was the year before I came."

"Then who lives here now?" Helen asked.

"No one, exactly," Jack said, taking a hand. "The school uses it as a sort of guest house. When Mummy came out for a fortnight last term, she stayed here, and Maeve Bettany's people did and a lot of others."

"You see," Meg Walton explained, "it's awfully hard to get lodgings on the Platz, because every room is taken up with relations of people at the San. Often and often, the school lets folk who simply must be close at hand have a room if there isn't anywhere else to go. But I don't think," she added, staring at the building, "that there's anyone there this moment. It doesn't look like it, anyhow."

"What's that?" Miss Charlesworth asked as she and Miss Ferrars came up with them. "Anyone in Unter den Kiefern? There certainly is not. They are having some repairs and painting done and it's empty at the moment. The men start work on Monday. That's why we came here this afternoon, because you won't be wanted in the least next week or the week after. The men won't want coveys of schoolgirls running round while they're busy."

"Doesn't the school ever use it now? For lessons and things, I mean?" Gillie asked.

"Not as a rule," Miss Ferrars informed her. "But we did that term we had the scarlet fever epidemic—do you remember, Miss Charlesworth? All St Mildred's and those of the two Sixths who had escaped came here until the worst was over. Unter den Kiefern was a blessing that term!"

"What are all those buildings over there?" Kitty Anderson asked, pointing to a long wooden erection of one storey which led to another of the same height.

"Those were the extra cubicles for the Millies," Arda Peik explained. "There were not enough rooms to take them all, so they built this. That part with just two windows is the passage so that they could go back and forwards to school during bad weather without going outside."

"Were there so many of them?" Gillie demanded, a curious look in her eyes.

"Nearly forty, I believe," Barbara said.

"Oh, just about our number," Kitty laughed in all innocence. Gillie darted a look at her but made no comment, and at that point Renata asked Miss Charlesworth if they might go in and show the inside to the St Hilda girls.

Miss Charlesworth shook her head. "Sorry; but I haven't got the keys. I didn't think of bringing them. In any case, all the furniture is under dustsheets in the

41

middle of the rooms, ready for the workmen coming in, so I'm afraid you wouldn't find it very interesting. But you may go and look in at the windows, if you like," she added in her usual easygoing way.

She had no need to speak twice. As one girl, the entire thirty-odd of them dived for the windows and stared eagerly, most of them chattering like starlings. Gillie, however, was silent. An idea had come into her head, and she was busy revolving it in her mind. She must discuss it with her own boon companions. If they thought it was a good notion, she might try it out on her elder sister Phyllis.

"If I can only slip into Phyl's mind to hint to Monica to talk it over with Miss Ashley, I shouldn't be surprised if she didn't do something about it," Gillie thought. "Anyhow, it's mad for the school to have this great place absolutely empty and forcing us to cram in with their girls. I don't suppose Ashey knows of this place, but I bet if she hears of it she'll try to bag it for us. I don't suppose she'll like being shoved in with the crowd of mistresses they have here any more than we like being shoved in with the crowds of girls. But I don't see how I can go and ask her about it. She'd only think I was being cheeky and tell me to mind my own business. I'll have to get on to Phyl and get her to see if Monny will do it."

"Don't you like it, Gillie?" Jack asked her suddenly. "You haven't said a word so far."

Gillie jumped and went red. "I—I was thinking about something," she said hurriedly. "Yes; I think it looks quite a decent place. Why didn't St Mildred's stay here?"

"Because it gets frightfully hot in the summer," Barbara, overhearing, informed her. "It's right in a little nook, you see, and shut in by the pines. I know they used to feel awfully limp sometimes in the hot weather. It's far fresher up on the Platz."

"Oh, I see," Gillie murmured. Then she removed herself as far from Jack and Barbara as she could. Jack's black eyes seemed to see right below the surface on occasion—or else she could make jolly good guesses. Barbara seemed to know things, too. Gillie had no intention of letting anyone from the Chalet School into her secret.

Miss Charlesworth gave them another five or ten minutes. Then she called them to order, told Meg to lead back this time, and when the long straggling line had been set going, followed with Miss Ferrars.

Gillie linked her arms in Mary's and Anne's and Kitty had to scuttle after them if she did not want to be left behind, Gillie set such a pace. They were very soon close up to Meg and her two companions, delicate Gretchen von Ahlen and a new girl, one Valerie Gardiner, who looked exactly what she was, a pickle of the first order.

Meg turned at the sound of the hurrying feet and halted the St Hilda girls with a cry of, "Hi! You can't go ahead of us, you know. We're the leaders, so you'll have to keep behind."

"Oh fiddle!" Gillie retorted. "We'll go ahead if we like!"

"No, you won't—not if you know what's good for you!" Meg retorted firmly. "Don't be an ass, Gillie! You'll only get into a fearful row and probably be cut off from the Evening. You don't want that, do you?"

"I couldn't care less!" Gillie snorted.

"What happens if you're cut from the Evening?" Kitty asked curiously.

"Sewing in Matey's room," Meg rejoined briefly.

"Sewing!" Even Gillie joined in the horrified exclamation.

"But that is what happens," Gretchen said. "It is not nice. Matey is cross because she has to sit there, also. And for the needlework, it is *schrecklich*!"

"What's that?" Kitty asked, staring.

43

"What is what?" Gretchen asked.

"What you said—schreck-something. What's it mean?"

Gretchen giggled. "It means horrible—not nice—disgusting!"

"Well, but sewing always is," Kitty stated her opinion flatly. "How is this worse than ordinary sewing?"

Meg grimaced. "It's turning sheets sides to middle; or hemming down the sides of ones done already; or making dusters or pillowcases—ghastly things like that. And Matey makes such a fuss about your stitches being neat and even! Oh, I know! I've had some!"

"What had you been doing?" Kitty asked with interest.

Meg giggled. "It was when we were in IIIb. Some of us had a squirt battle in the Splashery. Mary-Lou was Head Girl that year and she heard us and came and caught us and marched us off to Matey pronto. We were all more or less wet, of course, and some of us were drenched. We had to change and so Matey had to know all about it. Oh, how mad she was!"

"Matey?" Gillie asked, forgetting that she was at odds with the Chalet girls in the interest of this anecdote.

"Yes, of course. Mary-Lou only said we were little asses and sent us up to her. She knew all right Matey would tell us where we got off. She did, too. Then she dosed us all with some horrid cold medicine. Last of all she said we could spend the evening helping her with household mending instead of playing progressive games. It was Va's Evening, you see, and they had arranged some gorgeous progressive games, some of them quite new, with prizes and we were out of it."

"And," Gretchen put in, "Mary-Lou took all the squirts from you and never gave them back."

"Weren't you in it?" Kitty asked curiously.

"Gretchen was in San with swollen glands," Meg explained. "She was always having things like that the matter with her. She's lots better now, though." She suddenly glimpsed Valerie's face and gave a gasp of horror. "Val Gardiner! If you ever try to do anything like that, I'll never tell you another thing about us. What's more, I'll tell all the others not to tell you either."

"Oh, well, don't worry," Valerie said. "I haven't got a squirt, as it happens."

"Well, just you get one and try that sort of thing on me and you know what'll happen!" Meg warned her.

"Oh, all right! I say! I can hear the others coming. Hadn't we better get a move on?"

They moved on, Gillie and Co. falling behind a little, and finally reached the Platz where they had to line up again and end by walking demurely in pairs along the road to the school. No one said anything more on the subject. In any case, after tea—which the St Hilda girls were learning to call Kaffee und Kuchen—Miss Annersley sent for all St Hilda's except the two top forms and told them how they had fared in the tests.

Thanks to these, it had been found possible to spread the girls over a far greater number of forms. This was a relief to the staff, though a good many of the girls were far from pleased. For one thing, it broke up several chummeries. Gillie found herself left in Lower IVa along with Moira Baker and Helen Henderson, neither of them special friends of hers, while Kitty moved to Upper IVb and Mary Candlish and Anne Crozier were sent to Lower IIIa along with Susan Austin, Jane Mortimer and Anne Thorsby.

The same sort of thing had happened in the other two classes from St Hilda's. Phyllis Garstin and Katherine Rutherford, who had been placed for the time being in Inter V along with the rest of their crowd, found themselves in Vb while two other girls moved down to Upper IVa. Altogether, Miss Holroyd's girls found themselves pretty widely scattered over the five intermediate forms. As soon as she had told them what their various fates were, the Head sent them off to change for the evening.

When they came down to Hall, they found that they were to have games and country dancing. The Chalet School girls, well trained in the art of being hostesses, gave them no chance to sit about in corners either gossiping among themselves or feeling out of it. They were brought into everything and, if she had told the truth, even Gillie would have owned to enjoying herself.

Supper or Abendessen came at eight o'clock, followed by Prayers and then everyone below Form Upper IVb went to bed. This was the first intimation any of them had of the difference there would be, now that they were moved into so many different forms, and Gillie and Mary pulled long faces over it. It parted them from Kitty, and though that young person generally insisted on going her own way, she was one of their chummery and they didn't like the separation. However, there was nothing to be done about it—not with Jack Lambert shoving them into line to march up to the dormitories after they had said goodnight to Miss Annersley, who stood at the foot of the stairs, frequently adding a sentence or two to some girl.

When Gillie's turn came, the Head said, "How did you enjoy your ramble, Gillie? Have a good time, dear?"

There was nothing for it but to say, "Yes, thank you, Miss Annersley."

Upstairs, the duty prefects were in the dormitories making sure that everyone stripped off her counterpane and folded it neatly; reminding people to hang up their evening frocks carefully and, when the chatter rose too loudly, hushing the excited girls. But at last the bell rang for lights out, and the prefects left the dormitories and raced off downstairs to make the most of the time left to them. There came a few sounds of people turning before they finally settled down. Then silence fell.

Gillie had fully intended to lie awake and think out her

ideas in detail, once there was silence, but nature was too strong for her. What with the long afternoon spent in the open air and all the exercise they had had in Hall, she had been glad to scramble into bed and snuggle down under the blankets. As for lying awake, she found it impossible. Len Maynard had scarcely left the dormitory before Gillie's eyes closed and, whoever else might still be settling, it wasn't Gillie. She was sound asleep and she slept solidly all night and until the rising bell woke them next morning.

Chapter 6

MINETTE AGAIN!

"PHYL, can I speak to you a minute—please!"

Phyllis Garstin paused on her way to the lacrosse pitch where Ruey Richardson, the three Maynards and one or two other enthusiasts were waiting for those from St Hilda's who had begged leave to try the new game. Extra coaching had to be done in their own free time, so Phyllis was in a hurry. However, her young sister looked worried.

"What's wrong with you, Gillie?" she asked. "You look as if you'd lost half-a-crown and found a penny. Anything up?"

"Well, I've had an idea and I want to tell you and—and ask you what you think of it. It's—it's something for the school and—well, I thought p'raps you'd help me."

"Something for the school?" Phyllis's eyebrows shot up into her brown curls. "Do you mean St Hilda's? What are you getting at?" Then, as Gillie was dumb, she laid a hand on one thin shoulder and walked the younger girl off to the shrubbery. "Now," she said when they were reasonably safe from interruption, "you get cracking and tell me what all this is in aid of."

But now that her sister was listening, Gillie found it difficult to start. However, Phyllis was looking impatient, so she did her best. "Well, it's this way. Did you know that the Chalet School has another house?"

"Another house? What do you mean?"

"Besides all these up here, I mean," Gillie explained. "It's that place down at Welsen—isn't that what they call it?—a big chalet called Unter den Kiefern. Did you know?"

"Oh—that! I've heard about it, but I haven't seen it. What about it?"

"Well, it's empty. They aren't using it at all. Phyl, don't you think it would be a notion if they let Ashey and Miss Kent and Matron take us all down there until somewhere for always can be found for us so that we can be our own school still?"

Gillie had got it out at last. She stood back and gazed anxiously at Phyllis.

She saw nothing to encourage her in her senior's face. Phyllis was enjoying life at the Chalet School. She liked having all the extra competition in work. She had made one or two new friends already and she was looking forward to playing lacrosse. Above all, she had never hit it off with Miss Ashley, and she had a feeling that that young woman without the Head as a final court of appeal might be even more difficult to get on with than ever.

"What on earth put that into your head?" she asked. "I don't think it would be a good idea at all. For one thing, I don't suppose they have any school furniture down there, not to speak of books and stationery and all that. It would mean moving what we should want down for just the time we should be there and I don't suppose they'd agree for a second."

"They have furniture of some kind there," Gillie said. "We saw it, all heaped up in the middle of the rooms and covered with dustsheets."

"Yes; but I rather think I've heard that they use that place as a guest house. It almost certainly isn't school furniture. And another thing, it would make the lessons awfully awkward. Ashey and Miss Kent can't teach everything, you know, and I don't suppose they'd feel like engaging extra staff on their own without Miss Holroyd's permission."

"Wouldn't some of the Chalet School mistresses come down and help out?" Gillie asked, looking rather blue. This was something she had forgotten.

"Why should they when they can teach us in form up here without the bother of traipsing up and down in all weathers?

49

Of course they wouldn't! It would upset their whole timetable too. Where's the point of it?" Phyllis glanced at her watch. "Is that all you wanted to see me about?"

"You don't think it would be decent to be on our own again?" Gillie's voice was full of disappointment.

"I do not. Why do you want it, Gillie? Are you in a row of any sort with someone?"

"Oh, no!" Gillie spoke hurriedly. "It's only—well, I'd rather we were on our own. There's that big house going to waste and I thought it would be just the thing."

Phyllis laughed. "I'd advise you to think again, then. No one's going to upset present arrangements more than can be helped. I'm sorry if you've set your heart on it, kid, but I'm afraid it just won't work at present. Well, if that's all you want, I must run. Ruey and Len and the others are going to coach some of us in lacrosse and I don't want to lose a moment of it. See you sometime!"

She sped off, leaving a grievously disappointed young sister behind her and forgot all about it. Gillie stood for a minute, kicking at a pebble in the path.

"It's rotten of her!" she thought. "I guessed Monny would squash the idea, but I did think Phyl might be keen. Isn't there anyone who cares excepting our crowd?

"It looks as if I'll have to go to Ashey myself," she thought as she finally gave up the pebble and began to wander out of the shrubbery and across to the playing fields. "I don't know how that'd work. Ashey always has such a down on our crowd. She might take it as fearful cheek and she does say such nasty things when she thinks you're cheeking her."

She could see no way out of it, and it left her in an edgy state.

Gillie was hailed loudly by the rest when she joined them. She was wanted for shooting practice at netball, Heather Clayton having undertaken to give them coaching. Heather was second games prefect and very good all round. Lower IVa and b had been duly thrilled when she offered them half-an-hour or so. If St Hilda's didn't know, the Chalet girls did, that this was free time for Heather and they appreciated her unselfishness. Gillie, in a thoroughly fractious mood, didn't even think of it.

Matches of any kind with other folk did not begin until the following Saturday, so, since it was a fine day, they went rambling again that afternoon.

This time, Lower IVa and b went together and in quite the opposite direction from Welsen. Two mistresses went in charge of them and two prefects. One of these was Aimée Robinet; the other was Len Maynard, one of the sub-prefects. The mistresses were Miss Denny, who taught the very junior piano and also what Len had once called "an assorted bunch of languages", and Miss Moore, who took senior geography. Neither was very well known to the St Hilda girls as yet. Miss Moore was young, attractive-looking and very jolly out of school hours, though it was rumoured that she could be a tartar when she chose during them. Miss Denny was elderly, short, sturdy and plain, though her face was redeemed by a pair of twinkling brown eyes and the humour in it. Her chief claim to notice, so far as St Hilda's was concerned, was that she was the sister of Mr Denny, the somewhat eccentric singing master. He was known to the Chalet School as "Plato" though why nobody could tell them. Barbara said he always had been; Gretchen remarked that her mother knew, she thought, but she had never said anything. Meg observed that it was a mystery—none of which helped in the least.

The ramble started with something completely unforeseen. Miss Denny kept her eye on the school at large, and she had duly noted what was going on among the Middles. She decided that it was time something was done about it. When she sailed out to claim her string of girls, she took one look at the long lines awaiting her and set to work to make a few changes.

"Now then!" she said in her peremptory way. "This won't do at all. You've been together long enough to know something of each other. Let's change partners a little. You, child—Jack Lambert! Take this girl here." She moved Kitty out of her place and handed her over to Jack. "Wanda, take her partner. What are your names, by the way?"

"I'm Kitty Anderson," Kitty said, "and this is Gillie Garstin."

"Right! I'll soon get to know you all. Gretchen, you take this girl, and Margaret Twiss, you take her partner." And on she went down the lines, making changes to suit herself until every St Hilda's girl had a Chalet girl for partner and the two schools were thoroughly mixed.

Len and Aimée joined them while this was going on. Aimée was a black-eyed, black-headed Valaisian, who was art prefect and was reputed to be highly gifted in design. Len had chestnut hair and violet-grey eyes and was easily one of the tallest girls in the school, standing five foot nine inches in her stockings. She had been pointed out to Gillie and Co. as being "frightfully clever, but a complete poppet for all that". Now, as they watched Miss Denny, she and Aimée looked at each other and grinned. They said nothing and neither did Miss Moore, who stood to one side, smiling pleasantly and leaving her senior to it. Finally, having got them arranged to her liking, Miss Denny gave the word to start and they set off, through the Chalet School grounds and out by the back gate which led them directly to a meadow where, as Jack informed Kitty, they practised skiing during the winter sports season. Halfway along this, they turned right and presently found themselves at the foot of a steepish hill.

Miss Denny gave the word to break ranks and instantly the two schools separated. Gillie sent a compelling glance round her three chosen friends and the rest joined up in their usual clumps.

"Little idiots!" Miss Denny said disgustedly to Miss Moore as they tailed off the long procession.

"What else do you expect?" that young lady asked placidly. "It's really very hard for them, Sally. St Hilda's know they are only pro tem. and see no reason why they should become Chaletians when they're not and never likely to be." She added in a different tone, "What's that demon Val Gardiner up to?"

Miss Denny looked ahead and saw the bobbing red curls of Valerie making for the trees which bordered the hill path. However, someone else had seen too, and Len Maynard's voice was heard!

"Val and Celia! Come back! You can't try short cuts just here. You'll just have to keep with us and go straight ahead." The pair turned back, Val making a face.

"I told you so!" Celia said to her. "You pipe down, Val. I don't want to get into any rows, whatever you do."

"Well, I don't call it a ramble if you've got to stick to the path like glue," Valerie grumbled.

"Oh, don't be an ass!" Jack, who was near enough to overhear, interposed. "We've broken—and we're just jogging along as we like. Of course it's a ramble!"

Squashed all round, Valerie said no more and Len, with some idea of keeping that enterprising young person out of mischief, started them off on netball gossip, so the incident was forgotten. Aimée joined a bunch of St Hilda's girls and was chattering pleasantly about the nativity play which would come off that term. Gillie and her friends were going on ahead, their heads close together, and Gillie was doing the talking, though none of the others could hear what it was about. Once, though, Len, leaving Valerie and her crowd to run ahead and slow down three people who were too far in advance, heard Kitty Anderson say, "Oh, forget it, Gillie! What a stirabout you are!"

She wondered what was wrong and noted in her mind that Kitty's epithet was a just one. It exactly described

Gillie. Then she caught up with Arda, Heidi and Renata and cautioned them about sprinting on, before falling back to be greeted by Jack, who wanted to ask her something.

In due course they came to the little stream. There had been rain during the early part of the week and the rivulet was fairly full. The girls were delighted with it. They stood watching joyfully as the amber-coloured water went dashing down; here, breaking into tiny waves round a large stone; there forming miniature rapids over a pebbly reach; then brawling about the fallen trunk of a tree, part of which lay in the water. They turned down to follow its course, and came to a sturdy stone bridge, arched high above the banks.

"What's that for?" Kitty demanded.

Len, who was near, replied, "It's for motor traffic. The bridge down on the road is only a plank bridge and couldn't take the ambulances and our coaches. Besides the road narrows a lot there. They made a minor ring road up to this bridge—look!—and it drops here to the highroad again."

"It is full, isn't it?" Renata said, gazing at it hopefully. "If we had a whole day's rain, it would flood, wouldn't it, Miss Moore?"

Miss Moore laughed. "Not nowadays— at least, I hope not after the last bad floods. Don't forget the deep channels they dug further up to carry off excess water."

"Come along, girls!" Miss Denny's voice broke in. "No more loitering! Kaffee und Kuchen is early today, remember."

Most of them turned and went plunging down the path obediently. Only Jack, Wanda and Kitty lingered for a last look. Miss Denny paused. She knew better than to leave them to it. Miss Moore and the two prefects were with the others so they could come to no harm.

"Oh, how I love it!" Wanda sighed in her own language. The next moment, she gave a cry and pointed. "Oh, look! There's Minette over there at the other side."

"Crumbs! So it is! However did she get this far?" Kitty

exclaimed. "Miss Denny, mayn't we catch her and bring her home, please?"

"She might lose herself," Jack added urgently. "Oh, please, do let us, Miss Denny. She's an awful long way from home and she might easily get lost among the trees."

"How will you get across?" Miss Denny asked dubiously.

"Jump—like this!" And without waiting for further permission, Jack took a running jump and landed on all fours on the opposite bank. Kitty went after her before the stunned Miss Denny could check her, though she recovered in time to prevent Wanda from following.

"No, Wanda! Wait here with me! You two are very naughty—Oh, Len!" This last in tones of relief as Len Maynard came running back up the path.

"Miss Moore sent me in case anyone had had an accident and you needed help," Len explained. Then her eyes fell on the other two on the far bank, doing their best to capture Minette who seemed well aware that they wanted her in a hurry, and was enjoying herself, letting them come almost within touching distance of her before she skipped off a little further on.

"Minette!" she exclaimed. "And how did they get there? Oh, they jumped, of course! Shall I go and help them, Miss Denny? You go with Wanda and tell Miss Moore it's all right and I'll see to these two and Minette."

It seemed the best thing to do. Miss Denny marched off the disgruntled Wanda, who felt very cross because she hadn't been so quick as the other two, and Len sprang right across the stream which, mercifully, was narrower here, and joined in the chase of Minette.

The tabby was having a very good time. She would wait, eyeing them thoughtfully while they crept up to her, holding out their hands and calling her by endearing names. As soon as they were within reach of her, however, she would give a flirt of her tail, leap out of reach and then stand watching them again. Len declared later that there was a broad grin on her face!

Just how long this charming game would have gone on, there is no knowing, but the prefect was wilier than her juniors. She left them to coax Minette while she skirted round some bushes, watching her chance. Once more, the pair were almost within reach. Once more, Minette skipped away—and skipped into steady hands waiting for her. Len caught her firmly by the scruff of the neck, picked her up and tucked her into the front of her coat, buttoning it securely and leaving only the pretty tabby head with its touches of white on the muzzle peeping out.

"You naughty cat!" Kitty said as she came to tickle the lady under the chin. "Shall I carry her, Len?"

"No; she'll be safer with me," Len said, still holding the lady's scruff firmly as a precaution. "Come on, you two! There's no time to argue. Off you go—and mind you look out for snags."

They all set off as hard as they could pelt. Finally, they reached the school and went in by the side door.

"Shut it securely, Jack!" Len said breathlessly. "I'm taking this imp straight to Karen in the kitchen and asking her to see that she's shut up somewhere safe. How on earth she got so far away, I don't know."

"She must have followed us," Kitty suggested. "We'll have to look out for—Mercy, Jack! What's the matter with you?"

Jack was pointing to the foot of the stairs and looking as if her eyes would drop out. "Lo-look at that!"

They turned. A dignified tabby lady was just descending the last stair and, in the shock of the moment, Len lost her grip and the one she was carrying slid to the floor with a yowl.

Minette—their Minette—was safe at home all the time and the Minette they had brought back with them was a stranger!

56

Chapter 7

ENTER JOEY!

WHERE humans were concerned, Minette was a friendly pussy. It was far otherwise with members of the feline tribe. She regarded most of her own race with little or no enthusiasm. When it came to an utter stranger appearing on her own preserves, it really was beyond bearing and she let them know it.

Now she stood for about ten seconds, staring at the intruder as if she couldn't believe her eyes. Then she swelled out to nearly double her usual size, switching her tail furiously from side to side, before she uttered a shriek of hatred and hurled herself at the intruder.

The other cat was no whit behind her. She had been upset, anyhow, by all that had happened to her. She had been taking a leisurely walk as a lady had every right to do, when she had been seized on, carried off whether she liked it or not, bumped violently the last part of the journey and now had been dropped down to face another cat who, far from welcoming her, seemed to have every intention of slaying her. The visitor prepared to sell her life dearly. She too swelled out and answered shriek with shriek. The next moment, the pair were rolling about the corridor, locked in each other's paws, spitting, clawing, biting and using the most unprintable language for all they were worth. Fur flew in all directions, and for at least half-a-minute the girls were so stunned with the shock of having made a mistake and kidnapped someone else's cat, that they stood stock still and did nothing about it. Then Len came to her senses, snatched off her coat and did her best to fling it between the fighters.

It was impossible. The two were much too closely locked. They merely swore vehemently and one of them freed a paw

57

long enough to bestow a lengthy scratch on Len's hand. Len gave a yell, dropped the coat and sucked at her hand.

Kitty dived in on the instant, but she fared no better. In fact, in her hurry, she trod on a tail, evoking an even louder yowl from one of the combatants, who clawed her ankles with vim. As she retired with a shrill squeal, Jack, who had been watching her opportunity, swung down and managed to grab each of the warriors by the scruff of the neck, just as Karen, who had heard the sounds of battle as she came downstairs from her own room, arrived with a jug of water she had hastily snatched up. As Jack stood clinging to those scruffs, but unable to do anything more, the big cook rushed up and emptied her water over Jack's arms and the two cats which Jack instantly yanked apart. Len snatched one—which, she never knew—and bundled it up in her coat while Jack clung to the other and the fight was over.

That was the moment when Miss Denny, coming to see if the trio had returned safely to school, appeared on the scene. She brought up short, taking it all in—the dishevelled girls, the furious cats, drenched like drowned rats, Karen with her jug, the fur lying in tufts all over the floor. One Minette had a rapidly closing eye. The other was bleeding from a torn ear, and both were well-clawed in a dozen other places. Miss Denny was petrified for a moment. Then she spoke.

"What is the meaning of all this?" she demanded in no uncertain tones; and there wasn't the vestige of a twinkle in her eyes.

Jack, the ever-ready, told her. "Oh, Miss Denny, we—we've made a mistake! It wasn't our Minette at all. She was here all the time and when we put the other one down, she came and went for her. We've just managed to separate them."

"So I see," Miss Denny said. "Thank you, Karen. I gather it needed you to do it. I will see to the young ladies—and the cats," she added, regarding the casualties with some horror.

Karen said, "Danke, Fräulein!" picked up her jug, and departed.

"And now," Miss Denny observed, "are any of you girls scratched? You, Len—and Kitty?" as her eye fell on the blood staining Kitty's stockings. "What about you, Jack? Keep hold of that cat!" she added quickly, as Jack's captive began to struggle. "Here! Bring them along here. They must be shut up separately and then we can attend to them."

The pair were carried along the corridor and shut into separate form rooms after the mistress had seen to it that all windows were shut. They were locked in and Miss Denny took the keys in case of any accidents. Then she turned to the girls. "Go and take your things off and change your shoes. Then come up to my room and I'll attend to those clawings. Be quick, please!"

"Must I come?" Jack said. "I'm not hurt."

"I think you had better." It was all Miss Denny said, but it was quite enough. Jack scuttled off after Kitty; and Miss Denny, having seen Len vanish into the prefects' Splashery, went to the kitchen to beg hot milk to soothe the souls of the warriors, and also towels to dry them.

That duty finished and the two quite evidently calming, the mistress went off to the room she occupied on the occasions when she stayed on at the school and found the three girls awaiting her. She produced iodine and bandages; anointed the scratches liberally—whereby Kitty nearly danced with the smart—and after some argument from both her patients, found sticking plaster to cover the wounds.

"You can let me see them tomorrow," she said when she had finished. "You can't tell which of the pair scratched you and we don't want any trouble with septic scratches. I may add," she went on, "that your mistake is

59

excusable. Those cats might be identical twins. Just how you are going to decide which is St Hilda's and which the stranger, is beyond me at the moment. Open the door, please, Jack," as a tap sounded. "Ah, thank you, Gertlieb." This last to the maid who entered with a big tray. Miss Denny proceeded to set out an ample meal on the table at the window and then fed her patients.

"We must do something about the other cat," Len said, the atmosphere having warmed up considerably. "But how can we tell which is which? I could have sworn the one we found in the woods was Minette."

"Gillie might know," Kitty said doubtfully. "She and Mary are crack—er—very fond of Minette. Well, I'm fond of her myself. But I can't tell one of those two from the other."

"Very well," Miss Denny agreed. "Finish your meal, girls, and then go and change for the evening. When you are ready, Kitty and Jack, find Gillie and Mary and bring them to me and we'll go and see if they can solve the riddle."

"Where will you be, please?" Jack asked. "Shall we bring them here?"

"No; downstairs, outside IIIb door."

As a result, Miss Denny, stalking along to the door a little later on, found the five—Len had come to see the end of this silly adventure—awaiting her, clad in their pretty evening frocks. Kitty and Jack had hurriedly decided to say nothing of the cause for the summons to the other pair. As Kitty had said, they would certainly blow up at the idea of the precious Minette in a fight and it would be as well to leave Miss Denny to make the explanations.

"And let's hope," she added piously, "that they're dry by the time we get there. Mary would have forty fits if she saw them looking like they did after Karen got going with her water."

"Now, girls," Miss Denny said, not realising that two of her audience knew nothing of the earlier affair. "Come in quietly and don't rush them. Len, here's the other key. Go and fetch the other, please. *And keep tight hold of her!*"

At this injunction, Gillie and Mary stared at her. What on earth was all this about? Who had Len Maynard to keep tight hold of—and why?

Len vanished next door and Miss Denny, having opened the other door cautiously and switched on the light, shoved the girls in and then shut the door behind them, telling them to remain quite still.

Len appeared at that moment, a damp and battered-looking tabby cat in her arms. Seated on one of the broad window sills was another, busily licking herself. Gillie and Mary gasped and stood gazing from one to the other with dropping jaws. So much occupied with the cats were the six of them, that no one noticed that the door had been gently opened and a tall, dark woman, with dancing black eyes taking it all in, had also entered and now stood waiting to see what was going to happen next.

Gillie recovered her tongue first. "But—that's Minette!" she gasped.

"But Len Maynard has her!" Mary exclaimed. "And—and—oh, what has been happening to her? Just look at her ear! Oh, poor Minette!"

"Which is yours?" Miss Denny asked blandly.

"The one on the window sill!"

"The one Len Maynard's got!" The two cries came together.

"They can't both be yours," Miss Denny pointed out, while the intruder stuffed her handkerchief into her mouth and shook with silent laughter. "One is a stranger. The question is—which?"

"I'm positive it's the one on the window sill," Gillie asserted, going towards her. "Minette! Oh, and she's all wet! Whatever has happened to you, precious?" She tried to stroke her, touched a sore place rather roughly, and was greeted with a growl.

"No!" Mary cried. "The one Len's got is Minette. Let me have her, Len. She's our cat; not yours!"

She stretched out her hands to take Len's burden, but that young person warded her off. "Better not, Mary. I've got her comfortably, and after the lovely battle those two had in the corridor, I should think they're both sore with scratches. The thing we've got to decide is which is the school's and which is a total stranger. I can't tell. They're as alike as sardines in a tin. We rather hoped you two could decide. But it seems you can't," she added.

"But how did you get hold of another one?" Gillie demanded.

"Have Jack and Kitty not told you?" Miss Denny asked.

They shook their heads.

"Just said you wanted us here," Gillie said. "Oh!" as the full beauty of the dilemma dawned on her. "How simply awful! We can't see any difference and though Miss Holroyd might—after all, Minette's really her cat—she isn't well enough yet to be bothered about it, is she? What are we to do?"

Before anyone could reply, Minette on the window sill stopped washing, cocked her eye at the party and spotted her foe. She swelled up and emitted a long hiss. Len nearly let her burden drop as the other cat instantly replied. This was the point where the visitor decided to take a hand. Coming forward, she said sweetly, "Yes, it's a puzzle, isn't it?"

"Mamma!" Len exclaimed, still clutching her wriggling captive. "Oh, keep still can't you?" to Minette. "When did you come up? Are the babies with you?"

"I'll tell you everything presently," Mrs Maynard said. "At the moment, you'd better do something about this. Those cats are going to be at each other's throats in another minute. I'd put them into separate cages or hampers or something like that. Cages would be best, because then you could bring everyone concerned to look at them side by side without risking having them tear each other in pieces. But part them you must."

It seemed to be the only thing to do. Miss Denny sent Len off with one Minette to return her next door and ushered the others out of the room where they were with injunctions to be sure they didn't let the other Minette out. That done, she locked the door, pocketed the two keys and then, while Len was flinging herself on her mother, a spate of questions bursting from her, the mistress turned to the four Middles.

"You had better run along to Hall. I'll ask Miss Kent and Miss Ashley and Mrs Thwaites to come along later and see if they can elucidate the problem—yes, Jack?" For Jack's hand had shot up.

"Please, what does 'elucidate' mean?" Jack asked eagerly.

"Explain—solve the puzzle," Miss Denny said. "Run along, all of you." They went, and she turned to Mrs Maynard, who was trying to answer her daughter's queries. "Well, Joey! I'm glad to see you! Meanwhile, Len—" she nodded towards the direction the others had taken, and Len said, "Yes, Miss Denny."

"Just a moment, Len," Joey Maynard said. "I'm hoping for you three and Felicity at home tomorrow. Also Ruey. You can let them know and I'll fix it with the Head. The usual time. Now be off, you stork!"

However, before Len could move, someone came whirling down the corridor and the next moment Miss Ashley was there, demanding, "What is all this about Minette? I hope nothing has happened to her, for Miss Holroyd thinks the world of her and she is her cat. If any of those monkeys of Middles have been ill-treating her, I must insist that they be properly punished."

"My dear," Miss Denny said, "it's another of her own kind who has been doing the ill-treating. The girls themselves got badly clawed in trying to part the pair of them. But you are

63

just in time to help us, I hope. We really are in something of a dilemma." And she told the story as concisely as she could, Joey Maynard standing and taking it all in while her eyes also took in a good deal more about Miss Ashley.

"I've always said we ought to be in a separate house," Miriam Ashley burst out. "It's ridiculous to try to run the two schools in one. Where are Minette and the other cat?"

Miss Denny showed her the pair, and even she had to own that she was beaten.

"But what are we to do about it?" she asked fretfully.

Joey, who had been standing quietly by, now thought it time to introduce herself. "We'd better send word round about for anyone who has lost a cat to come and interview the pair and see if they can decide. By the way, I'm Mrs Maynard from next door—Freudesheim. You, I know, are Miss Ashley. Are you better now? I've been down at Montreux, but I had all the details from my husband, Dr Maynard. I'm sorry for all the worry you've had, as well as your injuries. But at least Miss Holroyd is improving now. As for those cats, we can only wait, I suppose."

Miss Ashley's face had cleared considerably. "Oh, if Miss Holroyd can have visitors soon, then that will be all right!" she said. "I can talk things over with her and ask her—"

Joey checked her quickly. "No, Miss Ashley. That, I'm afraid, is what you neither can nor may do. Visits must be purely social with no business talk. My dear girl," she added somewhat impatiently, "haven't you grasped the fact that Miss Holroyd will be much too weak for days to come to have to bother about a single thing? She must not be agitated at all."

"Oh?" Miriam said blankly. Then: "But in that case, what are we to do?"

Chapter 8

THE PREFECTS DISCUSS IT

MINETTE had certainly made matters much worse than they had been. Somehow, the story of Karen's drastic treatment of the two cats had got round and all the younger St Hilda girls were up in arms about it. The Sixths were above taking sides, of course; and Phyllis Garstin and her two friends, Katherine Rutherford and Roberta Thompson, only laughed and wished audibly they had been there to see it.

As for the Middles, they, of course, had any amount to say. On the Sunday following the battle, no fewer than five promising squabbles broke out among them. Various unpleasant remarks were made both to and at each other. By the evening, anyone might have seen quite a number of them passing each other with noses in the air or else grimacing violently at each other.

"Silly little idiots!" Maeve Bettany observed to Lizette Falence the next day as they passed a group on their way to the art room.

Lizette laughed and checked to listen. Barbara Hewlett, Jack and Wanda were walking back from geography in a parallel line with Gillie, Mary and Anne; and Barbara was commenting loudly on the stupidity of people who made as much fuss over a simple catfight as you would expect over an air raid. Gillie, not to be outdone, informed Mary in pitying tones that of course you couldn't expect girls who had lived so long abroad to know much about the proper way to treat poor helpless animals!

As soon as they saw the prefects, the six stopped short and went demurely on their way, but with noses cocked high at each other.

"But Maeve, what can we do?" Lizette asked when they were out of earshot. "This is shocking! So rude to each other!"

"Nothing at the moment," Maeve replied. "We can't exactly barge in on their silly quarrels. Even the Head can't do that unless they start fighting."

Rosamund, who had come up in time to see the performance and hear what the other two had to say, looked serious. "So long as it only stays at that sort of thing!" she said. "Pulling faces at each other, I mean."

Maeve chuckled. "What do you expect them to do—go for each other?"

"Certainly not! They aren't babies, though I must say they're behaving in a thoroughly childish way. But they mayn't stop at simple backchat."

"Then what are you expecting?" Maeve demanded as they reached the door of the art room. "I should say backchat was enough for anyone with that lot!"

"They may start to play tricks on each other," Rosamund said flatly.

"That would be nothing new," Maeve asserted. "Look at the awful things Jack Lambert did the first term she was here!"

"I know. That's just it." Rosamund was looking very worried.

"We'd better have a meeting tonight and see what we can do about it. I'd forgotten what mad things Jack and Co. can do, and I don't doubt that Gillie and her little playmates can do equally mad things," Maeve said. "We don't want any nonsense of that kind."

"Do you mean a full prefects' meeting?" Lizette queried. "Can we do that? Monica is Gillie's sister, you know. It will be—not nice for her, n'est-ce pas?"

"H'm! There is that. Well, look here. Let's call some of our own lot together and talk it over before we say anything to Monica and Mary and those other two. I like

Monica—Mary, too. I don't want to make things uncomfortable for them."

It was finally settled that they three, Monica Caird, Marie Zetterling, Aimée Robinet, Francie Wilford and Len Maynard should be taken into counsel before anything was said to the rest of the prefects. Their choice was restricted to these five mainly because the rest of the prefects were on prep duty or else having private coachings that evening.

As soon as the prefects' room was deserted except for themselves, Maeve demanded attention and then recounted what she, Rosamund and Lizette had seen that morning.

"We'd better do something about it," she wound up. "They're only talking at the moment; but if it's allowed to go on, they won't stop there. You know yourselves what wild things Jack Lambert can do when her dander's up. And she never stops to think. She just does things pronto!"

"But Jack has never done anything worse than other people since she got into such a row for tearing Margaret Twiss's tunic," Len protested. Jack was one of her lambs and she felt bound to stand up for her.

"That's true. On the other hand, she's never been fighting mad with anyone since, has she?" Rosamund pointed out. "If the sort of thing we heard this morning goes on, what's the betting that she will end by losing her temper?"

"And as for not doing mad things," Francie put in, "what about last term when she and some more of that crew charged into the five on the bridge over the brook and nearly sent that infant, Win, flying into the water?"

"I'd forgotten that," Len acknowledged. "Ye-es. It doesn't do to take Jack for granted at any time. But how can we interfere? I've heard nothing you could pull them up for. Have any of you?"

On consideration, no one had. At the same time, it was fairly obvious that if things were allowed to go on, there would be a flare-up of some size before many days were over. It was not a pleasing prospect.

"We'll have to do something," Maeve said. "I'm all for preventing crime if we can manage it. The point is, how are we to prevent it?"

It was a puzzle. The prefects knew that they could hardly call the Middles together and tell them to stop fighting over two Minettes—so far, Joey had not succeeded in finding an owner for the other one—nor could they, as Rosamund pointed out, call them to account for passing each other haughtily or talking at each other.

"I don't see that we can do anything but keep an eye on them," Monica said finally. "All of you, watch that crew, good and hard."

No one could suggest anything else, and there they had to leave it for the present; but no one was satisfied.

"Well, we'd better get down to work," Francie remarked.

She got her work and the others followed her example. Presently, Maeve looked up from her French essay to observe, "I like both Mary Murrell and Monica Garstin, you know. They've fitted in very comfortably with us. But honestly, I have no use for those other two—Doris Bratsby and Pamela Oliver. Why on earth they should have been chosen, I can't imagine. If I'd had any say in the matter, I should have voted for Jean Callendar and Hilda Matthieson. They really do seem to have a little sense. I'm jolly thankful that all prefects in this establishment are Head's appointments."

"Talking of St Hilda's prefects," Len said, "have any of them said anything to you about this business?"

"Not a word; and I haven't liked to say anything to them. All the same," Maeve sounded unusually serious for her, "if this sort of thing goes on, we'll have to talk it over with

68

them. Do you think we ought to even now? I mean they might be able to do something about their own beauties."

"I think—better not," Lizette put in. "They might not like it."

"If it was the only thing to do, I can't say that idea would stop me," Maeve returned. "Oh, I agree it's better not if we can avoid it. There's quite enough trouble between the kids of the two schools. We don't want it coming to us. But if it does come to that, I shall speak, whether they like it or not." Her chin went out in a way everyone knew.

"You know," Len said thoughtfully, "I'm inclined to think that half the trouble is that we're two different schools. It can't be awfully easy for them to have to try to fit in with our rules and so on."

Francie Wilford looked up, a gleam in her eyes. "If you really want to know," she said slowly, "it's my opinion that it's the attitude that mistress of theirs, Miss Ashley, takes that is responsible for part of it."

"Francie! What are you talking about?" Monica exclaimed.

"Just that. I was talking to Monica Garstin yesterday and she says that she has a feeling that if she can possibly prise them out of here, Miss Ashley will do just that."

"Oh, I daresay," Rosamund struck in. "But you don't tell me that Miss Ashley or anyone else is going to talk to Middles like that, whatever she may do about the prefects. No mistress in her senses would."

"She mightn't talk, but they might feel it," Lizette said.

"But little girls of that age?" Aimée protested in the fluent German they were all speaking, since that was the language for the day.

"Why not? Gillie and one or two of those others are quick," Rosamund returned. "Also, they lead the others."

"Well, that is something we can do nothing about," Lizette pointed out.

The sound of the bell for the end of Junior prep broke in on the talk and it had to drop, for ten minutes later the door opened to admit Mary Murrell and Pamela Oliver who had been on duty. Some of the Chalet School prefects followed them and work became the order of the day. But though Maeve was, to all appearances, absorbed in her French essay, at least half her mind was on the school's latest problem. Len, a keen student, had contrived to thrust it to the back of her mind for the time being, but Marie and Rosamund gave very languid attention to their schoolwork. It was well for them that the two Sixths worked on the assignment plan, or they might have come off very badly in lessons next day.

Later on, the Chalet School prefects talked things over with their friends but no one seemed to have any solution to the problem and meantime, unless any of the authorities were with them, the Junior Middles continued in their evil courses. Finally, Mary Murrell came to Maeve, with whom she was growing very friendly, to demand if she had noticed anything.

"Of course I have! I'm not blind," Maeve returned. "I'm glad you've spoken about it. Saves me the trouble of speaking myself."

"I don't like it," Mary said seriously. "What on earth has got into the little idiots? If they think they're upholding St Hilda's standard, the sooner I get our lot together and tell them what I think of their behaviour, the better! Honestly, Maeve, I've never known them to be like this. Miss Holroyd would be awfully upset if she knew."

"Just as well she doesn't," Maeve said. "All the same, Mary, she is making real headway now. I ran into Uncle Jack this morning and asked him about her and Naomi Elton and he said both were coming along nicely. Miss Holroyd's burns are all healing well and the real trouble now is that broken ankle, and that's something that must

70

be left to time. But as soon as she can move about, she'll be dashing along here to see how you're all getting on. At least, I know that's what the Abbess and Bill would do and I don't suppose her reactions are very different."

Mary's face had brightened. "Did Dr Maynard really say that?" she asked joyfully. "Oh, I am glad! It's the best news we've had of her yet."

"Oh, yes; he said it," Maeve nodded. "You know your mistresses have been along to visit her this week. Only short visits and just social ones, so to speak. I mean they weren't allowed to discuss business with her. But it's real progress, isn't it? Still," she added, laughing, "it means you'll have to put up with us and our little ways for the rest of the term."

"That won't worry me," Mary told her. "In fact, I'm very pleased about it. You know I'm going to read modern languages for my degree and since we've been here I've learned to speak much more easily and fluently. Mlle de Lachennais has made a big difference in my accent. I can see it for myself. In fact," she added, laughing, "I'm coming on so nicely, that I'm hoping that when I have got that BA, I may have a chance of coming out here to teach—at St Hilda's if I'm needed. If not, then here."

"Good luck to you! But about those Middles. We'll have to do something. They're still restricting themselves to saying rude things at each other and making faces whenever they think they're not seen. In fact, I've never seen such a variety of grimaces as I have this term. But they aren't going to stop there. Sooner or later, someone's going to put a match to the fire and they'll all go up in smoke. And all caused by two cats! It's the silliest thing I've ever heard of!"

Mary considered. "I rather think it began before that," she said slowly.

"I never noticed anything until that business. What started it off?"

But Mary refused to say. In her own mind, she was

certain it was Miss Ashley's attitude to the present situation which had really set things going, but she was too loyal to gossip about one of St Hilda's staff. She only reiterated that the catfight had been one of the finishing touches.

"They're all strung up over it," she said. "In fact, it's a regular vendetta now. Anything might touch off the explosion."

And then, something happened which drove the whole affair temporarily out of the minds of the majority of the Chalet School girls, even the Junior Middles.

Chapter 9

Miss Ashley Drops a Brick

"Who lives in that place over there?" Miriam Ashley demanded, with a wag of her head in the direction of the large chalet she and Peggy Burnett were nearing, on their way to the Görnetz Sanatorium.

Peggy glanced at the place and laughed. "That is—or was—the place where St Nicholas began a year ago. Now, of course, the youngsters are at the school proper with all the rest of us. It's also the home of the Dennys and Herr Laubach. St Nicholas only had three form rooms, two dormitories and the mistress's study and bedroom—oh, and her assistant's bedroom and the Matron's room. Those last four are small. Then there were two flats and a maisonette made out of what was left. The Dennys have one flat and Frau Mieders and her mother and sister the other. The maisonette went to Herr Laubach as I've said."

"Who on earth is he?" Miss Ashley asked curiously.

"Our former art master. He retired at the end of the summer term last year and, as he had no other ties, he decided to remain on the Platz. He's an old man—he was art master when I was at school and I'm no chicken," Peggy said with an elderly air.

Miriam Ashley glanced at her. "I don't suppose you're all that much older than I am. You don't look it, anyhow."

"Perhaps not. In any case, he wasn't exactly a youth when he came to us. I believe he's well on in the sixties. He hasn't been awfully fit lately, either," she added a little anxiously. "Usually, he visits the school every now and then, but so far he hasn't been near us this term and Mlle told me that he hasn't even been to Mass the past two

Sundays. That's why you haven't seen him—or heard of him, either, I suppose. I hope it's nothing really serious. He's what Mrs Maynard calls one of our foundation stones. Look, if you'll hang on a minute, I believe I'll call and inquire—"

She broke off short, for at that moment, Dr Maynard's car came swinging through the gateway with the doctor in it and he was looking very grave. He caught sight of the two young women and pulled up as soon as he was on the road, leaning out and waving imperatively. Peggy ran forward with a murmured, "Excuse me!" and Miss Ashley was left to dawdle after her.

"Dr Jack! Who's ill here?" Peggy demanded as she reached him.

"Herr Laubach; but I don't want you to talk of it or mention that you've seen me here. The school will know all about it soon enough."

"Why? What's wrong? He's not very ill, is he?"

"Dying," the doctor said curtly. "No; you can't do anything. Matey is with him, and Joey too. It won't be long, in any case, now."

"Oh, Dr Jack! How dreadful!" Peggy wailed.

"Don't look so upset, Peggy. He isn't suffering and he won't. He's quite unconscious and going fast. But Peggy, there's no need for anyone to know about it until the end. Say nothing to anyone—or you, either, Miss Ashley," he added, for Miriam had come up to them and had heard all this.

"Certainly not," Peggy agreed in subdued tones. "But can't anything be done? We don't want to lose him, you know. He's part of the school."

"Nothing—and, as I said, don't wish it. Where are you two going?"

"To the San. Miss Ashley is visiting Miss Holroyd and I'm going to see Naomi. She'll be upset when she hears."

"Say nothing to her. I'll tell her myself when the time

74

comes. But if you two are going to the San, hop in and I'll run you along. I'm going there myself."

Peggy and Miss Ashley scrambled in beside the doctor and he set off at once. They reached the Sanatorium which dominated all that end of the Görnetz Platz, and he dropped them at the gate, for they were going to the part of it that was given up to accident cases and the isolation wards. These were at the farther end of the grounds, well away from the wards where patients suffering from tuberculosis were. Before he left them, he warned them again about mentioning Herr Laubach's illness to anyone.

"We've promised that already," Peggy reminded him.

"I know. I'm just warning you again. You know how news goes round in a place like this. By the way, Miss Ashley, don't tire Miss Holroyd by too much business discussion. She's coming along nicely now. We're all very pleased with her and we don't want to have to start worrying about her again. It's only five weeks since the accident and she was very badly shocked. So be a little careful, won't you?" He flashed a smile at the girl.

"I'll be careful," Miriam Ashley said. "You may be sure we don't want her to have a setback. We're all hoping that she may be able to be with us next term, anyhow."

He had no reply to that. Miss Holroyd was making good headway, now that the worst was over, but he felt fairly sure that next term would see her still in the Sanatorium, even though the burns were healing nicely. However, no need to say anything about that for the present. He waved them off and drove up to the principal entrance while Peggy led the way across the short turf to the other part.

Once inside, they parted. Naomi Elton, a former pupil of the school, was now in one of the general wards. She had undergone two major operations as the result of accidents and for months had been condemned to lying on her back. Now, however, she was recovering and it was felt that she would be better among other people. Miss Holroyd was in a ward with three other people, two of whom were there as a result of mountaineering falls, while the third was recovering from an operation. This last lady was sleeping, but the other two were knitting and reading. Miss Holroyd, propped into a sitting position, was looking out of the window. At sight of her young mistress, she smiled broadly and held out her hand.

"Miriam! How nice to see you! Yes; I'm better—though I've still got to put up with this contraption on my leg." She waved her hand towards the awesome-looking structure which kept her leg stretched and weighted so that the bones should knit straight and true. "I don't mind owning that it gets wearying at times. However, the doctors all think that the bones are setting well and that, if I'm patient, I shan't have even a limp after a while. I can put up with dull toothache in my leg with that prospect before me."

"I should think so!" Miriam cried. "I'd no idea there was a risk of limping!"

"Well, there won't be, if I'm content to make haste slowly and keep quiet for the present," Miss Holroyd said comfortably. "Thanks to the Chalet School, I can do that. The girls aren't missing anything and you have a good home for this term, at least. I admit I should have done considerable worrying about you all otherwise. As it is, the work seems to be going on nicely, and from what Mrs Thwaites and Miss Kent tell me, you people are with a very jolly staff, which eases matters out of school hours. I may be very grateful for everything."

Miss Ashley was silent. So far, she had made little or no effort to become friendly with the Chalet School staff, though she knew that both of her colleagues had settled in happily. But then, they were content to accept any difficulties and make the best of things. She was becoming obsessed with her desire for a place where St Hilda's could be by itself. With only the other two and visiting

76

staff, she would have been an important person. As it was, she was just one of the younger mistresses and had very little voice in decisions that must be made.

Miss Holroyd turned her head to look at her. All she said was, "And which games are our girls taking up? Has anyone opted for lacrosse?"

"No; not so far as I know. The older girls play hockey and those under fourteen play netball. Apparently, it's the rule of the school that no one plays either hockey or lacrosse before she's fourteen and a half, so of course our girls have had to give it up for the time being. I think it's a pity, myself."

"I'm not so sure," Miss Holroyd said thoughtfully. "Hockey's a good game, but I've sometimes thought it was rather too strenuous for the younger girls. And, of course, netball is much better because they are more or less upright the whole time. You remember, Queen Elfrida's had the same rule about age."

"I'd forgotten that," Miss Ashley acknowledged. "All the same, Miss Holroyd, I do wish that we were on our own. It isn't always easy when our girls are so mixed up with the Chalet School crowd. Don't you agree that it would be much better if we could find a house somewhere and keep St Hilda's as St Hilda's?"

"But my dear girl, how can we possibly? You know what a time I had of it before I found the other place. And remember this. That though we are well covered by the insurance, it will be some time before we can hope to touch any money. When things are settled, we shall have to go slow for a time. It means starting from scratch again, for I suppose nothing much was saved from the holocaust?"

"I'm afraid not," Miriam said reluctantly.

"Then we may be very thankful that we haven't to worry about that for the present. In any case, I'm afraid I shan't be ready for house-hunting for some time to come.

Luckily, Miss Annersley assures me that they can keep us all next term and even all the summer term, if that should be necessary. In the circumstances, I think we're very well off."

"But Miss Kent and I could look round in our free time, couldn't we?" Miss Ashley urged. "And I can tell you something I heard of only this afternoon. The Chalet School owns a big chalet midway between here and the other end of the Platz. They used it for St Nicholas House, but now they've built the new place and the Kindergarten have been moved there. Of course, the part they used for the babies wouldn't be enough for us, and the rest of the place is divided up into flats and a maisonette. But the maisonette is let to an old art master of theirs—Herr Someone-or-other—and I heard this afternoon that he's dying, so it'll be free and surely we could manage with that addition. Don't you think it's an idea?"

Miss Holroyd looked at her, an odd expression on her face. "How do you know this?" she queried.

"Miss Burnett and I were coming here together and we met Dr Maynard coming out from visiting the art master and he told us."

In her excitement, Miriam forgot that Jack Maynard had asked them to say nothing to anyone. When she thought of it later, she salved her conscience by remembering that she had never given him any promise herself. She also raised her voice slightly and Peggy Burnett, coming in search of her, overheard her words and also her next sentence. "I simply can't see why the Chalet School should be able to hog all the spare houseroom up here to itself when we need a place, and with the school part and that maisonette too, we could manage quite well. I call it unbridled greed!"

Peggy felt furious. She nearly dashed forward to treat Miss Ashley to an unvarnished description of what she

78

was. Then she remembered Miss Holroyd and got hold of herself with an effort. A flaming row before the Head of St Hilda's would do that lady no good. Nor, if it came to that, would it make things any better for the two schools—and Peggy knew quite a good deal of the feud going on among the younger girls. If it grew really bad and Miss Holroyd had to hear of it, it might do her real harm.

"But honestly," she thought, as she stood by the door choking down the spate of angry words that nearly burst out from her, "this Ashley wench is the outside edge! Oh well, she's young, I suppose! It's to be hoped she'll get a little more sense as she grows older!"

But Miss Holroyd was replying and Peggy slipped back into the corridor. Not, however, before she overheard the elder woman say, "What nonsense! They don't 'hog' all the houseroom, as you say. And as for the spare rooms there, Miss Annersley told me herself that they would have offered it to us, but the quarters were far too small for our numbers. You forget that you can't crowd girls of fifteen and sixteen together in quite the same way that you can children of seven and eight. As for poor Herr Laubach's part, I don't know what you imagine it to be, but I can assure you it's only a sitting room and kitchen with two bedrooms and bathroom over and none of them of any great size. No, my dear. That is perfectly useless."

What else she may have said, Peggy never knew. She took another five minutes to get herself thoroughly in hand and then went into the ward again. Miss Holroyd was looking very determined and Miriam Ashley could only be described as sulky. Both looked relieved when the Chalet School mistress walked in to say, "Time's up! We must be getting back. The light's beginning to fail and we have to walk the whole way, remember."

Miss Ashley stood up. "I suppose we'd better go."

"We must," Peggy said firmly. "No one likes us to be out on the road after dark unless we have torches and there are a number of us. I certainly didn't bring a torch and I don't suppose you did. I'm sorry, Miss Holroyd," she suddenly remembered her manners, "but we must go. But you look as if you were convalescing at a cracking rate," she added with a bright smile.

"I am, thank you, though it'll be some time before they'll let me get up," Miss Holroyd said, turning from her mutinous mistress with some relief. "You are—?"

"Peggy Burnett. I take games and PT in the Chalet School. Some of your youngsters are awfully good," Peggy said. "And we're grateful to you for two good forwards and a very steady back in hockey for the First XI. By the way," she added, " some of your girls are anxious to start lacrosse, but we didn't like to agree without your consent."

"Oh, they have it," Miss Holroyd replied, laughing. "Who are they? But I mustn't keep you now. Come and see me some day when you can spare the time and we'll discuss it together. I'm always at home just now," she added with another laugh, in which Peggy joined.

"I'd love to. But we really must get off. I'll wait for you at the door, Miss Ashley," she continued. "Goodbye, Miss Holroyd. I'll come along as soon as I can. We're practically at half term, and once that's over, you never know what you may get in the way of weather."

They said goodbye, and Peggy departed to wait for her companion at the outer door. Miss Holroyd warned Miss Ashley again about leaving matters as they were for the present.

"You may be sure that as soon as I know how we stand and am able, I'll do what I can to find somewhere for us. In the meantime, you must make the best of things," she said briskly. "Now goodbye, my dear. Come and see me again some time. I like to have news now that I'm over the worst. Goodbye, now."

Miriam had no choice but to go, though she was far from being satisfied. However, Miss Holroyd was a little anxious about a long dark walk for the two girls, especially up on the shelf. She had visions of one or both walking over the edge and landing somewhere in the depths below.

It was a very silent walk back. Peggy led the way to the gate which opened on to the playing fields. It was a good deal of a short cut and, in this sort of light, much safer than the road. At the gate, they were met by Rosalie Dene, the Head's secretary, who was looking very sober.

"Where on earth are you going at this time of night?" Peggy demanded.

"To St Mildred's with a message for Bill. Don't keep me, Peggy."

"What's wrong with the telephone?" Peggy asked, startled.

"St Mildred's is out of commission. I'm going partly to let them know, but mainly to tell Bill and let her tell the Millies that—" Rosalie stopped short and swallowed hard.

"You mean—Herr Laubach?" Peggy spoke shakily.

Rosalie nodded. "He died half-an-hour ago. Jack Maynard rang and the Head will tell the girls at Prayers this evening. Don't say anything, will you, Peggy? Or you, either, Miss Ashley."

It was a great pity that Miriam Ashley had allowed herself to become so obsessed with her latest plan. She would never have said what she did then if she had been in her right senses. As it was, before anyone could say anything else, she exclaimed thoughtlessly, "So he's really gone? Then there ought to be a chance for St Hilda's with that place and we could be on our own again!"

Chapter 10

MARGOT THROWS A SPANNER IN THE WORKS

THE words were no sooner out of Miriam Ashley's mouth than she was wishing she had bitten her tongue out before she had spoken them. It did not need the shocked silence of her two companions to tell her that she had made a bad mistake.

"It's not my fault, actually," she thought. "It's theirs, snatching all the houses in the place and refusing help to people who really need it. And how can I be upset about an old man I've only just heard of?"

Peggy Burnett was prepared to air her views of the position unsparingly, but Rosalie Dene was too quick for her. She was older by some years than Peggy and in many ways more experienced. She spoke quickly before the younger woman could make things worse than they were.

"You'd better hurry off, Peggy. Tell Mlle where I am, will you, and say I shall probably have Kaffee und Kuchen with Miss Wilson. Scram!"

Peggy looked at her, shutting her pretty mouth into a thin, straight line. Then she turned without another word and ran off across the darkening field. Rosalie, left alone with Miss Ashley, turned to that young lady.

"Can you find your way back? It's not really dark yet and I must hurry off to St Mildred's, or I'd see you safely to the gardens. You can't lose yourself. Keep straight on till you come to the gap in the hedge and you'll come out by the shrubbery. You know the way after that, don't you?"

For the life of her, she could not keep the ice out of her voice. Miriam Ashley gave her an apprehensive glance, but she replied that she could find her way quite easily.

Rosalie noded to her and went through the gate with no more ado and Miss Ashley was left to trudge across the wide field, through the gap, and along the path which led to the house.

This was all very well, but worse was to come of it. Shortly after Rosalie left, Miss Annersley suddenly remembered a paper she wanted to send to Miss Wilson. She hurried after her secretary, only to be told that she had already left the building. Margot Maynard, her informant, added, "Shall I go after her and ask her to come back? I expect I can catch her up easily if I run."

"Yes—no. Wait a moment, Margot. I want her to take this paper to Miss Wilson. Put your shawl on and run after her. She's gone to St Mildred's and she'll have taken the short cut across the playing fields. Be as quick as you can, dear. It's getting dusk quickly now."

"I'll run all the way," Margot promised, taking the paper and skipping off to the Splashery to collect her big crimson shawl, which she tossed round her shoulders. She slipped out of the side door and went racing at full speed after Miss Dene.

Rosalie had walked briskly, but Margot quickly overhauled her. Rosalie reached the gate—and her two colleagues. Margot, a little behind, stepped back while they spoke and none of them noticed her. Thus, she overheard the first few sentences of the colloquy that followed, which was a pity.

Margot Maynard had a temper which, in her earlier days, had caused serious trouble for herself and a good many other people, though certain happenings had taught her a severe lesson and nowadays she had it more or less under control. But she had known Herr Laubach all her life and was fond of him—out of school, at any rate. Miss Ashley's unstudied remark made her see red and the only wonder was that she contrived to hold on to herself at that moment. It took a big effort, but she did it and took time to wonder what she should do about her errand. By the time she had decided to go forward, the trio had broken up, Miss Burnett hastening away while Miss Dene detained Miss Ashley for another minute or two. Then they parted and, while the latter sped off after Miss Burnett, the secretary passed through the gate and made good time along the path which led to St Mildred's.

Margot scurried after her at once, calling, "Aunt Rosalie! Aunt Rosalie!"

Miss Dene heard and stopped. "Margot? What are you doing here?"

Margot held up her paper and came panting to her side. "Auntie Hilda sent me after you with this for Auntie Nell," she gasped. "Will you please give it to her?"

"Thank you. I should have remembered it myself, I suppose. But it's dark now. Run back as fast as you can. You know you girls aren't supposed to be out by yourselves after dark. No," as Margot tried to speak, "never mind talking now—unless you have a further message for me. Go straight back and be quick about it, please. I'll see you some time this evening."

Thus ordered, Margot turned back and Rosalie, troubled enough already, forgot about her at once. Therefore, since no one had warned her definitely to hold her tongue, Margot marched straight back, tossed her shawl down anyhow on the lockers and made for VIb's form room, bursting in like a bombshell. Most of her compeers were making the most of what time was left before Kaffee und Kuchen to get on with their work. Some of them just glanced up to see who had come in and then went on with what they were doing. Only Francie Wilford, who had just finished her French essay and decided that it wasn't worth while beginning anything new, looked at her properly. What she saw made her sit up with a bang.

"Margot! What on earth's up with you?" she exclaimed

84

in startled tones, speaking in forbidden English, since this was German day.

At this, every girl present stopped work and eyed Margot. Her own triplet sisters recognized the signs at once. Len, the eldest of the trio, took steps.

"What's happened, Margot?" she asked anxiously.

Margot drew a long breath to steady herself. She had had time to realize more fully the inwardness of what she had overheard and she was raging. Every one of her red-gold curls was bristling with anger and her eyes were flashing blue fire. But she got hold of herself and she forced herself to speak quietly in the beginning.

"Poor old Herr Laubach—died—" she stopped there and choked, and the cluster of girls broke out into cries of grief and surprise—except, of course, for the St Hilda girls, who knew nothing about him.

"How do you know?" Len demanded. "And shut up, all of you! If you make a row like that someone will be coming to make inquiries. Margot, are you sure? Who told you?"

"No one did exactly," Margot said. "The Head sent me after Deney with a paper to take to Bill. She'd gone to St. Mildred's—to tell them, I suppose. I'd nearly caught up with Deney by the back gate, only Burnie and Miss Ashley were there and she was talking to them. I stood back, but I couldn't help hearing. And then, what do you think that beast Miss Ashley said?"

"Here! Not so much of 'the beast', if you please!" Hilda Matthieson said sharply. "Miss Ashley belongs to St Hilda's, please remember!"

"Sorry!" Margot said, most impenitently. "But she is a beast and even you will think so when you hear. Deney was all choked up—anyone could tell that by her voice—and Miss Ashley said, 'So he's really gone. Then there ought to be a chance for St Hilda's with that house and we could be on our own again.' Now then!"

There was a stunned silence. Margot's news, together with Miss Ashley's unfortunate exclamation, had taken their breath away and they were not very sure what to say. Betty Landon recovered herself first.

"Did she really say that, Margot? What a—what a heartless remark to make! He's only just gone and she had to start in on his house like that! And to Deney, who's known him since the year minus! You're quite right, Margot! She is a beast!"

By this time, the others had pulled themselves together and the room rang with their comments on Miss Ashley and her behaviour. Only Len Maynard held her tongue until, the hubbub increasing beyond reasonable limits, she checked it by clapping her hands smartly together.

"Stop it, you idiots! Do you want anyone to come and ask if we think we're Juniors still? Use your wits, the lot of you!"

That brought them up short. There was silence. Then Primrose Trevoase asked in subdued tones, "What else did they say?"

"Can't tell you. I told you I didn't mean to listen in and I backed at once. Anyhow, Deney sent the other two off and went herself. I did try to tell her I'd heard the first bit, but she wouldn't listen," Margot went on with an uneasy glance at her sisters. "She told me to hurry back at once because it was getting so dark. She left me after that, and I came straight back here." Suddenly, she swung round on the St Hilda girls. "Well, now you know, aren't I right to say she's a beast?"

In their heart of hearts all three agreed with her, but their loyalty to their own school and its staff would never permit them to say so publicly.

"I don't suppose she had the foggiest notion who he was, Margot," Hilda said apologetically. "I know we hadn't. And it's natural she should want us to have our own house and be a school on our own and not just part of another one. You can understand that, surely?"

"You've been awfully decent to us," Anne Crozier added, "but—well, it's not quite the same thing. I'm sorry Ashey talked like that, but I expect it's as Hilda says—she just didn't think. Anyhow, you can't expect us to call her names to you, can you?"

"Margot, just exactly what did Deney say?" Len asked. She was standing partly screening her other sister Con. Con was, so far, the only one of the Maynard family to show any signs of being artistic, and she and Herr Laubach had been great friends, even though he had more than once brought her almost to tears by his strictures on her work. Len knew well enough that behind her, Con was dabbing at her eyes and trying to control her chokiness.

Margot considered. "She said he'd died just half-an-hour ago and—O-oh!" Margot's voice became shrill with consternation. "Oh, I say! She said they weren't to tell anyone because the Head would tell us as a school at Prayers. Oh, gosh! And I've given it away myself!" She stood stockstill for a moment. Then she whirled round and made for the door.

"Where are you going?" Len cried.

"To tell the Head what I've done, of course!" And Margot disappeared on the word, leaving the others staring at each other in dismay.

"What on earth do we do now?" Betty Landon demanded.

"Only one thing to do," Len said quickly. "We say nothing to anyone, of course. We aren't supposed to know and we shouldn't if Margot had thought. We can't tell anyone or mention it until the Head's told us herself. You do understand that, don't you, Betty?" with a stern look at that young person, who had a name for being a gossip as well as one of the most inquisitive girls who ever wore the Chalet School uniform.

Betty flushed. "Of course I do. You needn't look at me like that, Len."

"The rest of you agree?" Len turned to the others, after a nod to Betty.

They all did and, mercifully, the gong sounded before anyone could say anything more and they had to hurry to put their books away and go to the Splashery to wash their hands. They were joined there by the other members of the form, who had been busy with special coaching, music lessons or, in the case of two of them, remedial exercises. No one mentioned Herr Laubach, but their peers found those of them who knew strangely distraught, and Con Maynard kept well away from the others. However, all who knew her were accustomed to that. Even now, when she was old enough to know that she must keep her imagination in check during school hours, Con was subject to odd fits of silence and absence. They thought that she was off in her own magic world and let her alone in consequence.

Margot came late and looked very subdued. No one could say anything just then, but later on she refused to answer any questions, though she did confide in Len that the Head had flattened her by asking if she had any idea of taking a leaf out of Con's book and blurting out everything regardless of consequences. However, as a result of her interview, a message came from the Head to Maeve Bettany, the Head Girl, bidding them go straight to Hall when their meal had ended. Miss Annersley had decided to tell them the sad news about Herr Laubach at once. The way in which it was received told those St Hilda members of VIb who were in the know just how badly Miss Ashley had erred in saying what she had said.

What was even worse, although the members of VIb kept that piece of information to themselves, it created a split in the form. The Chalet girls voiced their opinion of the mistress fully and freely, and the five St Hilda girls who were with them in form felt they must do their best to stand up for her and did so, Doris Bratsby even going so far as to insist that it really was a natural thing for the mistress to have thought of the possibility of having the house when you came to think of it. Hitherto, the feud had been kept up mainly by the Middles. Now it broke out in VIb. It looked as if the entire school would be embroiled in it before it ended. Naturally people of fifteen and sixteen were not going to behave as the younger girls did; but the pleasantly friendly atmosphere which had obtained among the elder girls up to that time had vanished so far as VIb was concerned. Everyone was very polite—stiltedly polite, in fact. Their manner to each would have done credit to a Victorian seminary for young ladies. But there was nothing pleasant about it and it would not be long before VIa and then the staff noticed it, and then anything might happen, as Len Maynard said worriedly when she was talking it over with her own special cronies on the Sunday.

Chapter 11

THE HOBBIES CLUB

THE school's grief at the death of Herr Laubach caused the feud to die down gradually, at least among the elder girls. The senior St Hilda girls realised how much he had meant to the Chaletians, and by common consent Miss Ashley's thoughtless remarks were no longer referred to, then forgotten in the excitement of half term expeditions. Among the Middles though, the feud still bubbled under the surface, and finally came to a head again.

It was largely Jack Lambert's fault—hers and Gillie Garstin's. The pair were very much alike and they got across each other in the most shocking way. Both were dominant characters, leading their own followers by the nose. Both had hot tempers, though Jack had hers more under control than Gillie had. At the same time, when Jack did lose her temper, she was apt to say and do things she would never have thought of in her normal moments.

As Monica Garstin said to Len Maynard on one occasion, they were born to be either bosom friends or bosom enemies. "And which it's likely to end in," she concluded, "is more than I can see. Of course, Gillie being so much the youngest of the family, she's been rather spoilt at home."

"So is Jack much the youngest of her family," Len said with a grin. "I rather think, though, that they're not a spoiling family. We can't do anything about it, Monica. They'll have to fight it out between themselves. I only hope they don't burn down the entire school before they end it!"

Among other activities of the Chalet School, was the Hobbies Club. This began very early in the school's history—in fact, when Joey Maynard was a Middle. The St Hilda girls were enchanted with it. They found that all sorts of handcrafts were open to them, for the girls went in for a variety of hobbies. Among the Seniors, quite a number made lace of various kinds. Others were keen on chip carving, pottery, weaving, and woven beadwork. The Juniors made scrapbooks of a superior kind, for they were untearable and washable; they also made toy animals, and dolls' clothes. All of them, with two or three exceptions, knitted; and all the continental girls embroidered. They dedicated the results of most of their efforts to their annual Sale of Work in aid of the free wards at the Sanatorium. They met on one evening in the week and enjoyed themselves thoroughly.

When she first came to school, Jack had been a problem. She was very much a tomboy and the interests of the others came in for wholesale scorn from her. She loathed needlework and her sewing lessons were purgatory for all concerned. Her efforts at art would have disgraced little Felicity Maynard. Pottery, weaving, basketry—she treated the lot to ineffable sniffs. She was happiest when she was fiddling with machinery, up to the eyes in grease and dirt; and her fingers, which were so clumsy with a needle, could operate cogwheels and ratchets with the utmost delicacy and precision. Her great ambition was to become a charter pilot and her only collection was of pictures of aeroplanes and cars.

It may be imagined with what difficulty a hobby had been found for her, but finally Joey Maynard solved the problem by showing Jack how to cut jigsaw puzzles with a fretsaw—her own hobby, incidentally—and starting her off with a supply of wood, pictures and glue guaranteed to stick for ever.

The school had a treadle fretsaw and Jack quickly learnt to manipulate it. In the previous term, she had taken up cutting models and found that even more entrancing. She produced a small wheelbarrow and, if the wheel joggled considerably, it worked after a fashion. During the holidays she produced an old-fashioned carrier's cart, complete with linen tilt. Her parents had provided a magnificent birthday present in the shape of a treadle fretsaw of her own and she had come to school determined to produce an aeroplane she had found in the book on fretsawing her brother and sister had given her.

Most of the St Hilda girls, after getting over their first thrills about the club, settled down to various activities. Quite a number of the elder girls pleaded with their own kind to show them how to make lace. One or two took up weaving, and others found basketry and woven beadwork appealed to them most. Kitty Anderson improved on the scrapbook idea. She begged to have the framework of a screen made and Gaudenz, the school's handyman, had produced it cheaply enough. Fine canvas was stretched over it and then Kitty began to turn it into a scrap screen of the kind popular when her grandmother was a girl. Two or three of the others were charmed with the idea and volunteered to help. They had piles of magazines begged from everyone and rolls of wallpaper from which they cut flower wreaths to form borders and frames. Miss Yolland, the art mistress, had given them a few hints about arranging their pictures and, after six weeks, they had finished one leaf of the screen and very well it looked. Gillie had been one of them, but she was not really interested. Like Jack, she preferred something to do with machinery, and she was extremely bored with it. This evening, when the others called to her to come and help cut out pictures, she shook her head and said airily that she wasn't bothering any more.

"But why not?" Mary Candlish asked, pausing in the middle of cutting out a Georgian lady with delightful hooped skirts and powdered hair. "Oh, come on, Gillie! I've got some decent pictures of animals for you. You like doing those, don't you?"

"Not me! I'm browned off and I don't care if you never get the old screen done!" Gillie snapped at her.

"What will you do instead?" Anne Crozier demanded.

"Oh, I don't know. I'm sick of cutting out and pasting, anyhow. I'm going to try something else."

"Well—what?"

"I've told you I don't know. I'll take a look around and see."

"No, Gillie! That, I fear, you cannot do," said Carmela Walther, one of the prefects in charge of the Junior Middles. "You would be in the way."

"Well, may I watch Jack?" Gillie asked in German of the most British kind.

Before Carmela could answer her, someone wailed that she was in difficulties with her knitting and the prefect had to go. Gillie went to the far side of the room where Jack was very busy, cutting the fine struts for her aeroplane. It needed great care not to snap them, and she was too much absorbed even to glance up when Gillie pulled up a chair and sat down beside her.

"Is it awfully hard?" she asked presently, as Jack paused to adjust her work and take a peep at her instructions.

"Not really," Jack replied, intent on her book. "You start with something easy, of course, and you have to be careful about your treadle or you break your saw blades. I began with jigsaw puzzles—cutting them into large pieces, you know, and it's awfully easy to cut too far and then your knobs break off." She pushed the book aside and returned to her treadle.

"What are you making?" Gillie pursued, helping herself to the book. "This? But it's an aeroplane—of sorts. Will it fly? How do you manage that?"

"Speak German," Jack warned her. "You use elastic, of course. The book says it'll fly. I have not tried it before—don't touch!" she added hastily in English. Gillie had laid the book down and was turning over the carefully cut pieces Jack had put into a box.

No one knew how it happened. Perhaps Jack's sharp exclamation startled Gillie. Perhaps the box had been put too near the edge of the nearby table. However it was, it tipped up and the bits and pieces showered to the floor. At the same moment, Gillie shifted her feet hastily out of the way and stamped firmly on one piece which crunched and broke. Jack sprang to her feet.

"You clumsy idiot! Why can't you get something of your own to do and not come bothering and ruining other people's work? Clear out of here before you do any more damage! Go on—scram!"

She flung out one hand in a furious gesture and caught Gillie on the ear. It was Gillie's turn to leap to her feet, her own temper flaming. "You needn't hit me!" she snarled. "I'm going! I wouldn't stay with such a beastly fusspot for two minutes! Making such a fuss about a bit of wood!"

"But Jack—Gillie! What does this mean?" It was Carmela who had come striding across the floor to where the pair stood, looking like two young turkeycocks prepared to give instant battle.

"It's her fault!" Jack was raging and she spoke without thinking. "All my evening's work ruined, just because she can't keep her hands off things!"

"Jack! Be quiet!" It was all Carmela said, but there was something in her voice that checked the spate of words on Jack's lips.

"Sneak!" Gillie shouted. "Telling tales—"

"And you be quiet, also, Gilbertine!" Carmela felt that strong measures were indicated, so she used Gillie's full name, much to that young woman's fury. But it certainly worked so far as hushing her went. She stood stockstill, her grey eyes blazing with anger and her lips set in a thin line.

94

The rest of the room was deadly silent. Everyone had stopped work and was staring at the trio standing there. Carmela turned her head with its coronal of black plaits.

"Go on with your work, everyone," she said quietly. They turned to it immediately. Carmela's discipline was always excellent—the more so, perhaps, because she rarely exerted it to the full.

Jack had gone scarlet at the epithet Gillie had shouted at her. Now she said, "Please, Carmela, I did not mean to tell tales. Please, will you take no notice of what I said."

"Certainly not!" This was Carmela at her stateliest. "I am not concerned with the cause of this childish quarrel. Go back to your seat, Jack, and continue with your work. Gillie, come with me. Why are you not working yourself? You should not have been interfering with another girl's work."

"Well, I asked you if I could watch her," Gillie muttered.

"And I did not say that you could. You should have gone to the work you usually do and asked me later on. You work with Kitty, nicht wahr? Why are you not with her tonight?"

"I—I—" Gillie stopped short. How did you say, "I was browned off" in German? She compromised. "I did not wish it," she said.

"Why not?"

"I didn't."

Carmela felt they were getting nowhere. She sent Gillie for her library book and told her to read for the rest of the period. It was quite clear that that young woman was in a state to fight with her own shadow and the prefect had had quite enough of that already.

Jack spent the time in carefully testing everything she had already cut and found that, apart from the piece Gillie had broken, they were all safe. The bell rang for Prayers as she laid the last one down. She was still feeling ashamed of what she had said to Carmela so the anger had drained out of her, though she had no friendly feeling for Gillie. Still, she must apologise. It took a good deal of swallowing, for Jack hated saying she was sorry. However, she knew it must be done. In her anxiety to get it over, she made straight for Gillie when they went to the Splasheries to wash the glue, paste and other messes off their fingers, and blurted it out.

"I say, Gillie! I'm sorry I hit you—that was an accident. And I'm sorry I said anything to Carmela about it, but I did feel so mad after all my evening's work being smashed up like that. But that's all right. She won't take any notice of it—well, you heard what she said yourself."

It was hardly a soothing apology. In fact, it was scarcely an apology at all, but it was the best Jack could do in the circumstances.

There was an expectant silence in the Splashery. Everyone looked at Gillie, but she was too full of her own grievance to notice. "If that's what you call an apology, you can keep it!" she growled. "And I may as well tell you now as later that I mean to go in for fretwork. I can make things as well as you, and I shall."

"But—but there is only the one treadle machine," Wanda von Eschenau said. "How will you manage? For Jack always has it, as she is the only one of us to like fretwork."

"Then she can just give it up to other folk sometimes and not go hogging it all to herself!" Gillie snapped.

"But—but aren't you going on helping us with the screen?" Kitty cried. "Why on earth d'you want to change like this in the middle of the term?"

"Never you mind! It's no business of yours!" Gillie told her rudely.

"But of course it's my business—our business. We said we'd do that screen together and it was all arranged!" Kitty snapped back.

"Oh, shut up! I'm sick of the lot of you!" Gillie had a whole kennelful of black dogs on her back by this time.

At this point, it seemed good to Margaret Twiss to remark to no one in particular, "Is this the sort of manners they have at St Hilda's? How ghastly rude!"

Naturally, every St Hilda girl present was up in arms, even though a good many of them thought Gillie was being outrageous.

"Our manners are as good as yours!" Mary Candlish flung at Margaret.

"And I quite agree with Gillie. Jack didn't even say decently that she was sorry for sneaking." This was Anne Crozier's effort.

Some of the others joined in and, before they knew where they were, almost every girl in the Splashery was involved. They made so much noise, that they never heard a quick step outside and it was a genuine shock when Maeve Bettany appeared among them, looking the complete Head Girl for once.

"What is the meaning of all this noise?" she demanded in her fluent German. "And why are you not speaking in German? Have you forgotten what day this is? Pay your fines into the box, every one of you, and never let me hear you breaking rules wholesale like this again. No!" as two or three tried to explain to her. "You may all be silent. I want to hear nothing more from any of you. Be quick and tidy yourselves and form into line by the door."

There was nothing for it but to obey. On the whole, Chalet School Middles would almost rather get into trouble with the Head than with the prefects, and the half term among them had taught the St Hilda girls the same lesson. Even Gillie in her present raging state held her tongue. As for Jack, she finished drying her hands and scuttled to take her place looking like a whipped puppy.

When the last girl had tailed off the line, Maeve marched them off to Hall where they took their seats for

Prayers in anything but a prayerful mood. Maeve, looking grimmer than anyone had ever seen her before, waited until Heidi Zinkel, the last, was in her seat and then stalked up Hall to take her place in the school choir. Her cousin Len Maynard could have told them that Maeve was in a bad temper when she looked like that, but the Maynards were with the rest of the Catholic girls in the gym and missed it. They heard all about it later when the prefects were assembled in their own room. Maeve gave tongue with a fluency that lasted full five minutes. When at last she stopped, Margot Maynard, who had no business there, since she was not a prefect, but who had come to ask a question about Maeve's mother, her Aunt Mollie, broke a stunned silence by saying, "Well, you ought to feel a lot better for having got all that off your chest. And now, may I have Auntie's letter, please? I haven't seen it yet." And Maeve was so startled, that she handed over the letter without any comment, and Margot got away with it for once.

As for the Middles, the thought of paying their centimes into the fines box helped to calm down most of them quite considerably. They went up to bed in subdued mood and nothing further happened that night.

Gillie and Jack, however, were both too furious to be cooled, even by the loss of some of their precious pocket-money. Gillie slammed into her cubicle and they heard her stamping about. Jack, grievously offended by what had been said about her apology—after all she said she was sorry!—was not far behind her. When Len Maynard, the prefect on duty, came up to switch off the lights, the atmosphere in her dormitory was thick and it was the same in the other dormitories.

Nor was it any better next day. Gillie's friends backed her up and told her Jack Lambert ought to be ashamed of herself for telling tales to Carmela.

Not that they got any change out of Gillie, who was at

odds with all her world just then. She knew that she had behaved badly in not accepting Jack's very lame apology and she felt herself in the wrong. Moreover, Kitty, who took things very light-heartedly as a general rule, was offended because her chum had, as she said, let them down over the screen, and refused to have anything to do with her. Anne Crozier agreed with Kitty, once she had time to think, and told Gillie roundly that it was her own fault for walking out on them like that. Very soothing for Gillie!

As for Jack, she sulked perseveringly for half the day. Then something happened which turned her thoughts in another direction. The day had been very grey, which had not surprised anyone, as the three previous days had been stormy, with continuous rain and high winds—could this have been partly the cause for their behaviour the night before?—but it had broken dry that morning. Shortly after fifteen hours, Jack, looking out of the form-room window, forgot that she was on her dignity and angry with several people. She uttered a squeal of delight.

"Mais regardez, tout le monde!" she cried, remembering to speak French. "Regardez la neige qui tombe vite!"

Everyone turned to stare out of the windows and sighs of utter rapture sounded from most of them. It was snowing and snowing hard. The feud was forgotten for the time being as they thought of tobogganing, skiing and snow-fights, and even Kitty brightened up, which was a relief. A cross Kitty was something very rarely seen, and her friends had felt even more depressed than before at the spectacle she had presented earlier in the day.

"If only it lies!" Jack breathed. But for that, they must wait and see.

Chapter 12

JOEY CREATES A FURORE

NEXT morning there was a general rush to the windows to
see if the snow was lying or not. Some very long faces
were pulled when the girls gazed out on grey skies
lowering over seas of mud and slush.

"Comme c'est effroyable!" Ghislaine Touvet cried.

"But," said Rosamund Lilley, who was prefect of her
dormitory, "you'd only to look at those great, wet flakes
falling yesterday to know that this would happen. Snow
like that never lies."

"Mais pourquoi pas?" asked Moira Baker, causing a
slight sensation among the other St Hilda girls in the
dormitory. No one had ever expected Moira to come up to
scratch in French.

Rosamund beamed on her before explaining that, first,
it was very early for snow in Switzerland. Second, the
snow that lay was the fine, dry snow like powder, and it
wasn't cold enough for that yet.

"How cold has it to be?" Helen Henderson queried with
a shiver. "I call this cold enough for anything."

"En français, Helen," Rosamund said firmly; and
proceeded to help her to find the French and then say it
with rather less English in her accent.

When Helen had accomplished this, it was her turn to
bath and she went off feeling cross. You didn't want a
French lesson to begin your day. Later, however, she
decided that after all it hadn't been wasted time, for she
did know that remark by heart. So did the rest of the
dormitory. In fact, the whole of St Hilda's was beginning
to speak both French and German with very much more
fluency than they had ever had before.

They came downstairs to find all lights on, but the rooms were warm and cosy, for Gaudenz and his henchmen had been at work on the heating early that morning. Things looked very much brighter, and there were surprises coming to them that day, though they did not know it just then.

The first hint they got was towards the end of Frühstück when the Head's bell rang from the high table. The under-current of conversation ceased at once and everyone turned to see what was wrong. Miss Annersley was standing and she was smiling broadly at them.

"I am very sorry, girls," she began, speaking so slowly and clearly that even the worst novice in French could understand most of what she said, "that we are condemned to yet another day indoors. However, it can't be helped. When it clears up again, you shall have a long morning in the open air. In the meantime, as there can be no walk, you may take the time to begin your preparation for tomorrow until Prayers. Work hard this morning, for we have something new for you this afternoon. That is all for the moment."

She sat down again, but her announcement had certainly brightened the general outlook. Even Gillie who had come down looking very gloomy, cheered up and when the rest of Lower IVb began speculating as to what was in store for them, she joined in, though she carefully avoided having anything to do with Jack Lambert.

It was at Break that they got the first hint as to what was coming. Len Maynard, standing with her sisters near a window in the Senior common room while they made away with their chocolate and biscuits, gave an exclamation.

"There's the car—and Papa in it! Goodness! He's handing out something to Gaudenz!"

"Oh, what?" half-a-dozen voices cried, while their owners crowded round the Maynard girls to look out.

Maeve called them off. "Come away from the windows and don't stare like that. No; you can't go dashing to

Uncle Jack, Margot. Anyhow, he's getting back into the car and you're too late. I expect Auntie Joey has sent something along. It's time for the bell, folks. Better go and round up the kids."

So that put an end to that. But the Maynards were not the only ones to have noticed the advent of Dr Jack, as the school at large called him. Quite five form rooms looked out on to the drive and a number of people wondered why he had come since, so far as they knew, no one was ill.

The next hint arrived in the form of notes to all mistresses teaching during the last lesson that morning. The girls were to have their rest as usual, but when it ended and they had set Hall in order, they were to stay there, taking their usual places. The Head would speak to them.

In the excitement that this caused, everyone forgot to grumble because they might not take their usual run on the playing field at the end of school.

"What has the Head got up her sleeve?" Betty Landon inquired.

"Go and ask her," Margot advised.

Betty grinned. "I can see myself! No thank you!"

No one talked much during Mittagessen. No one wanted to wait any longer than could be helped for the Head's announcement. Even the staff were keen to know, for the Head had kept her own counsel and flatly refused to answer any questions.

"I'll tell you while the girls are resting," she had informed them. "Until then, you may hold your horses like the girls."

So they were left guessing, too.

After Mittagessen, the tables were cleared in short order and the girls scurried along to Hall for their half-hour's rest. It was just as well that no talking was allowed during this period, or the great room would have rung. Everyone was wildly excited and it is on record that Arda Peik looked at her watch twelve times during the half-hour!

As they settled down, Len Maynard suddenly gave vent to a weird sound and grimaced violently at Con who was beside her. Con stared at her thoughtfully for a moment before chuckling softly, all of which was highly aggravating to the rest of their clan, but nothing could be done about it then. Thus, when the Head entered Hall as soon as the bell rang, everyone was agog to know what was coming.

"Now!" she said when she had signed to them to sit down. "This morning, Mrs Maynard sent round the book of the nativity play. You will have your usual lessons for the first hour of afternoon school. Then you may do preparation for the time left. Change before Kaffee und Kuchen, please. As soon as you have finished, clear the tables and then go quietly to Hall. Mrs Maynard has sent typed copies of all the principal parts, so the mistresses and I are going to read it to you. Tomorrow, the parts will be given and rehearsals will begin on Friday evening."

A storm of clapping greeted this announcement and she let them have their heads for two full minutes before she held up her hand for silence.

"One other thing!" she warned them. "Please remember the rule. Anyone who behaves badly during lessons will not join us this evening. School—stand! Lizette, please!"

Lizette went to the piano, and the school marched off to the tune of a rousing march to do the best it could with lessons and preparation for what was left of the afternoon.

When they were upstairs changing into the velveteen frocks which were their usual evening attire, most of the dormitory prefects seized the opportunity to impress on their charges the need for eating and not wasting time chattering during Kaffee und Kuchen.

"Have we to be silent altogether, Len?" Wanda von Eschenau asked.

103

"No; but don't gossip," Len replied. "The sooner it's over, the sooner we shall hear the play and I'm longing to know what it is this time."

"Do you not know—really?" Jack demanded.

"My mother never tells us anything about it beforehand. How could she? It would be very unfair to the rest of you. So I'm as anxious to hear as any of you."

Thus warned, Kaffee und Kuchen took place in unusual quietness, and when the bell rang for the end of the meal, the girls sped to Hall where Miss Dene already was busy at the lectern on the dais.

As soon as the last Junior had taken her seat, Maeve Bettany went to ring a handbell, and the mistresses followed her when she returned. Some of them held sheets of paper and the girls guessed that these were the people who were to read the parts. Miss Annersley came last in a pretty green woollen frock with a white cardigan over it, for even with their central heating, Hall was apt to be cold in weather like this. She took up her stand by the lectern and smiled at the girls before she spoke.

Her first words brought relief to the St Hilda girls.

"The play is, as usual, in English. After Prayers, which will follow immediately after the reading, you may speak in your own languages this evening."

Everyone clapped and Miss Annersley laughed before she said that the reading would begin at once and left the lectern to take her seat in her big William-and-Mary chair, while Miss Wilmot pushed the lectern to one side. Then the play started.

It delighted the schools. Now and then, Hall rang with their laughter, for there was a good deal of fun in the play. Once or twice, they broke into clapping at a specially effective speech. For the most part, however, they remained quiet and eagerly listening. Now and then came pauses when little Miss Ferrars, the play's producer, rose to explain, "Here, you sing a carol." —"There's a dance here."— "This part is all miming."

When she had said this, a small voice rose from among the

Juniors to demand with stunning clearness, "Please, what is 'miming'?"

Miss Ferrars smiled down at the small fry and explained. "It's acting without any speaking, Felicity."

Seated at the back of the long rows of girls among the other Seniors, Margot leaned across Ted Grantley and Katherine Rutherford to hiss to her sister Con, "Oh, isn't that like Felicity? She always has to know on the dot!"

That was the only real interruption. The girls were mostly too enthralled by the prospect before them to want to break the thread of the reading. But when it finally ended, and before anyone else could move, Phyllis Garstin forgot her dignity and jumped to her feet, crying, "Oh, how simply marvellous! Cheers, everyone, for Mrs Maynard! It's a—a—a wonderful play!"

Chapter 13

HELPING GAUDENZ

"FIRST it sleets; then it rains! I call this disgusting weather!" Mary Candlish was standing by one of the common room windows when she made this statement. It was early afternoon of the Wednesday and there was good reason for her complaint. During the early morning, the great, soft white flakes of snow had been transformed into rain which was falling in a heavy downpour.

Jack and Barbara, also standing by the window, grimaced. "It's the sort of weather you can expect up here in November," Barbara said. "Didn't you have it wet in Geneva?"

"We did, of course." Kitty standing beside Mary put in her oar. "But we did think that up here it would be cold enough to make snow and not rain."

"No." Jack growled. "Oh, I'm so sick of being stuck in the house! I wish it would be fine for a change. I want to go out!"

She was not the only one. They were all tired of being housebound. As a result, they were also ripe for any mischief that turned up. However, all that did arrive just then was Mlle de Lachennais and the three people she had summoned to help her carry their work along from the sewing room. Something had gone wrong with the lights there, so needlework was to be taken in the common room for once.

"You may talk if you do not speak too loudly," Mlle said when everyone was settled. "Our story may wait until next week." She beamed benignly on them and the sulky faces smiled at the permission.

"Oh, thank you, Mlle!" they chorused as they set to work.

Talking was permitted with the Seniors as a rule, but for the most part, Mlle and her coadjutors found it well to keep the

106

Juniors and Middles quiet by reading a story to them. This was an unexpected treat and duly appreciated.

The awful weather, combined with the excitement of finding that quite a number of them had speaking parts in the nativity play and that the people responsible for allotting them had shared out important characters equally between the two schools, had made them forget their feud for the moment. So the girls mingled cheerfully together. Jack and her chums formed a group made up of Gillie and hers, with red-headed Valerie Gardiner and her pal, Celia Everett, thrown in for makeweight. Incidentally, it also consisted of some of the naughtiest girls among the Middles. Mlle had regarded it dubiously, but finally decided to let it go for once.

The Chalet School insisted on every pupil learning to sew whether she liked it or not. This term, Lower IVb had been set to making waist petticoats for themselves. At the moment, they were being taught how to set gathers into a band, and Jack and Co. loathed it. On the whole, Mlle thought it just as well they had decided to sit together.

"I wish we didn't have to sew!" Gillie muttered crossly as she struggled to arrange her gathers evenly to her band. "I simply loathe it."

"No more than I do, I'll bet!" Jack grinned, putting in her last pin and holding the thing up to see if it would pass muster with Mlle. She had already done it three times. "I say, anyone, do you think it's even all round now?"

Arda cast a glance at it. "It's better than the last time," she said. "Perhaps Mlle will pass it and let you tack it."

Mlle, making her rounds, came up in time to catch the horrible face Jack made at her friend and exclaimed, "But Jack!"

Jack went red. "Sorry, Mlle," she murmured.

"But it is to Arda you should say that," Mlle told her. However, she did not pursue the matter. She knew Arda too well. Instead, she examined Jack's work and told her that she might tack the gathers in place. The next moment, she was exclaiming at Mary who had calmly pinned both sides of the band over her gathers with an idea of saving trouble.

"But Mlle, why may we not do that?" Barbara demanded.

"Because, my child, you stitch the gathers into place with running stitch. Then you turn the other edge of the band over and hem that."

"It seems an awful waste of time," Barbara sighed, beginning on her tacking.

Mlle laughed and moved on to the next. Presently, she had finished with them and went to another group.

"How I loathe sewing!" Jack grumbled.

"I call it cruelty to dumb schoolgirls!" Anne Crozier agreed. "I'll never like it."

"Perhaps not," Mlle, who had caught this, turned to smile at them. "But every woman should know how to sew. Who knows? Some day you may live in a place where it is impossible to buy new clothes when you need them. Then you will be glad that you have learned how to make and mend, also. Persevere, mes petites!"

"Where in the world could you live where you couldn't buy clothes?" Celia inquired. "If there weren't any shops near you, you could surely have them posted."

"You might not," Renata replied. "You might be —might be—on a ship in the middle of the sea!" she wound up triumphantly.

"Or you might be living right up in the mountains somewhere—oh, not here, of course!" Gillie joined in. "But supposing you were—well—in the Andes?"

"Send by radio to the nearest town," was Jack's solution.

"If you were in the wilds like that, you mightn't have a radio—not a sending one," Kitty pointed out.

"You'd most likely have one like they have in Australia," Anne Crozier said. "Don't you remember in our last geography lesson what Ferry told us?"

"Oh, well, I don't know then," Jack returned.

"You might be shipwrecked on a desert island like the Swiss Family," was Wanda's brilliant idea.

"Oh, yes!" Kitty caught this up. "And you'd be there for years and—"

"I should think I'd have outgrown my clothes by that time," Jack said with a chuckle. "Besides, nowadays they know all the islands and they'd find me."

Renata finished her tacking and bit off the thread before she made a new proposition. "You might marry a poor man who couldn't afford to buy you many new clothes and be glad to be able to make them."

"That wouldn't happen to me, anyhow. I'm never going to be married. I think it's a lot of rot!" tomboy Jack retorted firmly.

Renata, nearly a year older, shook her head and Arda exclaimed, "But then, Jack, would you be an old maid? You can't wish that!"

"You bet I do! You don't catch me having to run a house and do all the mending and look after the babies and all that!"

Arda looked horrified. "But don't you like babies? I hope when I marry I'll have four—two boys and two girls. I shall call the boys Rudi and Adriaan and the girls Marie and Roosje—and the girls shall come here to school when they are old enough," she added.

"No one may ever ask you. You're counting your chickens a bit soon," Jack jeered. "Anyhow, I'll see to it that no one ever asks me."

"There's Gaudenz going past!" Kitty interrupted her. "What on earth is that great tin he's carrying?"

"I can guess," Celia said with a wag of her brown head. "My sister Audrey told me that someone had told her that he was going to varnish the doors beside the kitchens because he can't get on with outside work."

"Wish he'd let us help him," Jack grumbled. "I like

messing about with paint and varnish—oh, and putty! Putty's lovely stuff! Daddy did our garage this summer and he let me help him quite a lot."

By this time, Gaudenz and his can had disappeared and they returned to their hated sewing. They knew all too well that unless a certain amount was done, Mlle would appear at the end of their prep and take them off to make up for lost moments—not a good idea for their free time.

They contrived to satisfy Mlle's demands by the end of the period and then they all fled to change into shirts and shorts for gym, where Miss Burnett, with an eye to their lack of exercise, gave them a strenuous time which shook the fidgets out of them for the next two or three hours.

Next day, however, when they woke up to find that the rain had ceased, only to be followed by a furious gale, their discontent rose. Great gusts of over sixty miles an hour put a stop to any idea of their going out, even though the sun was shining. Indeed, the staff were thankful to remember that the last of the passageways linking up former outside rooms to the rest of the school had been completed during the past summer holidays and no one need even cross the courtyard at the back. The Middles, of course, never thought of that and they grumbled loudly and as fluently as they could in German, the language for the day.

"Never mind," Len Maynard said, overhearing a bunch of them complaining. "At least the wind will dry up the mud and when it dies down, we'll be able to have games and quite likely a ramble. As it is, we should have you all being blown off the Platz into the valley below, and I suppose you don't want that to happen, seeing you have no wings—as yet." Her eyes danced. "I shouldn't advise it, anyway." She went off laughing, and they looked at her resentfully. It was all very well for people like Len who liked to swot and liked to read; but it was rotten luck for folk like themselves who preferred to be on the go

110

outside. Even Jack, who as Margot Maynard had once profanely remarked, regarded Len as only a little less than a seraph, was moved to wonder aloud why older people got so dull!

"You'd better keep an eye on your lambs, my dear," Nancy Wilmot told Miss Stone, one of the new mistresses, who was Lower IVb's form mistress. "They're all sizzling with discontent and when that happens in this establishment—look out for squalls!"

"You alarm me! However, I'm not on duty with them either this afternoon or tonight. Miss Yolland has themfor art this afternoon and it's one of the prefects tonight, so you'd better warn her." Linda Stone laughed in Miss Wilmot's face and went off to give German Diktat to Upper IIIa.

However, the squall foretold by Miss Wilmot came when everyone was off guard and, once the first reactions of the school had passed off, enchanted them and became a worthy addition to the many school legends.

In one way, it was Gaudenz who was to blame in the first instance. He had worked on the doors all day—he was rubbing in linseed oil since, as they were of polished pine, they needed no varnish—and, instead of taking his can of linseed oil back to the shed whence it came, he remarked to Karen that the wind was wilder than ever and pushed the great can into a space in one of her store cupboards, ready for the morning. His wife was housekeeper for St Agnes, the farthest of the Houses, and they had three rooms in an annexe, so that he did not need to leave shelter at all. He went off and Karen, having seen that the evening meal was cooking in the great, slow- burning ovens and that all was as it should be in her kitchen, switched off the lights and went to enjoy a gossip with some of the other domestic staff in their pleasant sitting room.

Left to themselves, Lower IVb began to settle down to their usual ploys of reading, jigsaw puzzles and games.

111

They were Senior Middles now, though the lowest form in Senior Middles, and they were expected to need less supervision than their juniors. In any case, they all knew better than to indulge in noisy games at that hour. Only the malcontents found no amusement and clustered together. The truce was still holding and, in fact, most of them had completely forgotten the feud.

"What shall we do?" Mary asked. "It's all so dull!"

"Let's take a stroll round the corridors," Jack proposed.

"May we?" Gillie queried doubtfully.

"Well, we aren't exactly supposed to," Barbara owned, "but there's nothing to do. It'll be all right if we don't disturb anyone, I expect."

They were quite willing to believe her. They left the common room in a body and tiptoed down the corridors, finding some relief for their restlessness in moving about. Presently they came to the door leading to the kitchen regions.

"Let's go and ask Karen if we may have the two Minettes to play with," Kitty suggested.

No one had ever turned up to claim the second Minette and the pair had become reconciled to each other, ate together, played together and even slept together, now that the winter cold was coming. Karen had provided each with a collar, one blue, the other crimson, so that it was possible to distinguish them. They were great pets, but the girls only saw them at intervals. Kitty's idea was acclaimed in whispers and Jack pushed open the door and they went through.

Once it had swung to behind them, they relaxed their precautions a little. Unless they began to shriek, no one would hear them but the kitchen folk, and they chose to believe that they had a legitimate reason for being on what was forbidden ground, since they were seeking the cats.

"But how good it smells, nicht wahr?" Arda remarked, still contriving to speak German—of sorts. "I do like the smell of a kitchen."

112

"Oh, so do I!" Anne Crozier declared, sniffing rapturously.

Jack led the way down the narrow passage. They paused to admire the two gleaming doors Gaudenz had done. Then they went up the three steps which led to Karen's domain. They found the place in darkness, but they switched on the lights and looked round. Neither of the Minettes was there, both being in the mistresses' sitting room.

"Where are they?" Gillie asked. "Oh, surely no one's been brute enough to put them outside on a night like this?" In her dismay, she spoke English.

"Talk sense!" Jack retorted, abandoning her own efforts at German. "I expect they're in the maids' sitting room. Well we can't go there. Karen would shoo us off like nobody's business. What shall we do now?"

"Could we look round?" Mary asked. "I've never seen a kitchen like this before. What are those great things over there?"

"Those are the ovens," Wanda said. "Tante Marie has one like that in her kitchen. We do not, we live in a small house in Salzburg, but Tante Marie lives in a Schloss."

"That's the fridge," Barbara said, pointing to another big affair. "And over there is the door to the boiler-room. I've been in here before. Like to look?" She ran across the kitchen to throw open the door and they came crowding round her. There was nothing much to see, for the big boilers were closed down until Gaudenz made the rounds just before he went to bed, and even now, excited as they were, they dared not try to open a door. Gillie did suggest it, but a modicum of prudence remained with Barbara and she refused.

"What are all these cupboards?" Valerie asked.

"Karen's stores, I expect," Jack said. She tried a door, but Karen kept most of them locked.

A little further on, however, Valerie had found one

113

which was open. They peered in. On the shelves at the top were cans of polish, piles of dusters and polishing-cloths and other cleaning materials. Below was a rack for brushes and mops and standing on the floor was Gaudenz's great can of linseed oil. In another corner were two or three smaller cans, pushed there by a careless maid, and that was where their downfall came.

Pointing to them, Jack remarked, "Those'll be what Gaudenz puts his varnish in. He'd never lug that huge thing around."

"It isn't varnish, anyhow," Mary said, having removed the stopper to investigate. "It's oil of some kind. Ugh! What a nasty smell!"

"Oh, I don't think it's so bad," Gillie said, sniffing. "Take a niff, Jack. It's not bad at all, is it?"

"No; but he certainly won't be varnishing with oil," Jack said. "I expect it's something Karen uses. No; those are the cans he'll use for varnish. Daddy always puts his varnish into old tins because they're easier to shift." She looked round, a sudden gleam in her black eyes.

"But what are you thinking, Jack?" Wanda demanded.

"I was just thinking," said wicked Jack, her face alive with mischief, "what a shock Gaudenz would get tomorrow if he found, say, two extra doors done."

She had no need to say more. With one accord, they swooped down on the tins. Kitty and Barbara rootled till they found two or three brushes and they left the kitchens, all in a fine state of giggles.

Valerie did have the sense to switch off the light as she left the kitchen. Barbara had already shut the cupboard door when they had removed the four cans and the brushes. They were not to know that Gaudenz put his oil into a deep bowl, though they might have seen it if they had looked.

The brushes were handed out to the first five and the rest, stifling their chuckles as well as they could, awaited

114

their turn. They found it delightful work, though the "varnish" was a good deal stiffer than Jack, at least, had expected. They painted it on as far up as they could reach. Gillie wanted to bring a couple of the kitchen chairs out for them to stand on, but once again Barbara's sense led her to forbid it and Gillie subsided, being mollified by the offer of Jack's brush. So absorbed were they, that they never bothered about the time until the sound of the school bell ringing for the end of prep reached them faintly through the door. Then they woke up with a vengeance.

"Quick! We must get the cans and brushes back at once!" Jack exclaimed.

"But we cannot." Wanda pointed to the line of light that had appeared under the kitchen door. "Karen is in the kitchen."

"Lawks!" Gillie gasped. "What do we do now?"

They were in a nice quandary. They dared not face Karen. What was more, they were all realising that "sticky" was no word for them.

"We'll have to leave them out here in a corner," Anne said. "Perhaps Gaudenz will think he forgot them himself."

"Talk sense! He isn't daft!" Jack told her gloomily.

"Well, what are we going to do then?" Mary asked.

"Leave the things here and own up if there's a row," Barbara said. "It's all we can do. Push them into that corner so's no one will fall over them and then come on. We've got to wash."

"And we must hope that no one will see us leaving here," Arda supplemented.

This they contrived to do, but they had a rush to wash their hands and faces and sponge sundry drips off their frocks and yet be in time to take their places in the long procession marching into the Speisesaal. They just managed it, and more than one of them was unaccountably flushed when they took their seats. It is certain that someone would have noticed and made inquiries as to what they had been doing. But before she sat down after Grace, Miss Annersley announced that people with speaking parts in the play were to meet their several directors in various places for a "read-through" of their episodes after Prayers. Thereafter, no one troubled about anything but the play, which they discussed solidly throughout the meal, and the doings of the naughty girls of Lower IVb bothered nobody—until the morrow.

Chapter 14

Consequences

GAUDENZ was a giant of a man, germanically fair, with kindly blue eyes and a huge moustache. During the six years or so he had worked at the Chalet School, he had established for himself an unrivalled reputation for amiability. In fact, some people said openly that they doubted if he had a temper at all. The exploit of the previous evening was to put an end to that idea.

He began work at six, most mornings of the week. First he opened the great furnaces and raked them through, for they were still wood-fired. There had been talk of switching on to the electricity, but Gaudenz himself refused to hear of it. If a fire went out, you could always relight it; but electricity was another matter. His first job finished, he set off to go the rounds of the radiators. Now and then there was an air-block and it was his pride that only on one occasion had there been any really bad stoppage since he had taken over.

Since he knew the way from the kitchens to the corridor blindfold, he never troubled to switch on the light in the passage. The first thing that happened was that he stumbled over one of the tins the girls had hastily stacked at one side of the kitchen steps. This one had toppled off the others and rolled a little way, and Gaudenz nearly measured his considerable length over it. The passage itself had not been used at all the previous night.

Gaudenz staggered and just saved himself from sprawling. He reached out a ham of a hand and switched on the light. Then he picked up the can and looked at it disapprovingly. His look was more than disapproving when he saw the others.

"Ach! Idle hussies!" he ejaculated in his native Schweizerdeutsch. "They find it too much trouble to put the cans away! I shall speak of this!" He collected the cans, carted them into the kitchen where he dumped them on Karen's spotless table-top and went to wash his hands which had become sticky in the process.

Gaudenz had a slow-moving mind. He wondered what the maids had been doing to leave sticky cans about. Karen never allowed such a thing. He set off once more, intent on his duty. On the way, he paused before the first door to admire his work. The wood gleamed golden in the light without either smear or smudge. It was the same with the next one. He glanced at the next when he reached it. He would begin work here this afternoon.

The next moment, he was standing stockstill, his eyes starting. The wood glistened—as far up as thirteen-year-old arms could reach. But this was no work of his. Whoever had put the stuff on—and he would swear that it wasn't linseed oil!—had painted it on with no regard for the run of the grain or smoothness and evenness. There were smears and smudges in plenty here. In some places, the stuff was thick and lumpy. In others, it had been so thinly spread that the wood, which had been washed previously to rid it of all the old oil, showed blatantly through. And in parts, it had trickled down on to the floor.

For a moment, Gaudenz stood staring. Then, with a smothered roar, he rushed to the fourth door to find it in the same condition. The others had not been touched. Who had done such a thing? Who had dared to interfere with his work? And what had been used? He put a big, horny finger on the first of the maltreated doors and found it unbearably sticky. And that was where he finally blew up.

It would not be any of the kitchen folk—they would never have dared. It must be some of the young ladies.

Young ladies! That was not what Gaudenz called them in his mind. His blue eyes emitted sparks and his great moustache stiffened into tusks at the ends, so furious was he. There was only one thing to be done. He must speak to somebody at once! This sort of thing must be stopped immediately!

He thundered down the passage, flung open the door leading into the corridor and found all in darkness. Muttering furiously to himself, he switched on the nearest lights and clumped along to the office, turning on lights as he went and muttering all the way. The rising bell began to ring when he was halfway there, but he took no notice. He was so full of rage, he never realised that it was rather too early for Miss Dene to be about downstairs. So when he reached the office and flung the door open after hammering on it, only to find it still dark and empty, he almost literally foamed.

Back he thundered to the kitchen where Karen and her myrmidons were assembling, and Karen was already berating the culprit who had set sticky cans on her beautiful table. The maids were all denying the charge, but peppery Karen was not heeding them.

"I care not who has done it!" she stormed. "Sticky cans on my table or anywhere in my kitchen I will not allow! Take them to the scullery, and make them clean, Anneli. Then put them in their proper place and come here to me. I will know who has done this before I do another thing!"

"Well, it was I, so you need not blame the girls for that!" Gaudenz bellowed. "But what I will know is who is the worthless, lazy hussy who has left them in the passage so that I nearly fell on one. You would not have enjoyed it if I had broken an arm or a leg—no! Nor would you have enjoyed facing the gnädige Fräulein when she asked how it happened. There would have been tears, I make no doubt, and someone would have been sent off in disgrace. Who did it? Who did it, I say?"

He poured forth his grievance and Karen went with him to examine the doors and nodded shrewdly. "As for the cans, I cannot say. But this is the work of some of the little girls. See how the painting stops just there. That is as far as a child could reach." She paused to dab the wood and then sniff at her finger. She tasted, and a broad smile spread over her face. "Ach! Now the cans are explained. Taste for thyself, man, and then come with me. A cup of coffee, and then go and speak to Madame in her study."

Karen's treatment calmed the furious man considerably. When he went back to the office, he was even grinning broadly to himself, though he looked grave enough when he entered to find Miss Dene at work, sorting out various papers. The communicating door into the study was ajar and the light there was also on, showing that Miss Annersley, too, was at work. From all sides came the hum of noise, which showed that the school was up and some of it already at work.

Rosalie Dene looked up with her usual pleasant smile. "Good morning, Gaudenz. Anything wrong?" she added, for she had never seen their amiable henchman look as he was looking just now.

"I wish to speak with the gnädige Fräulein Annersley," Gaudenz told her. "And I wish to speak with her now. It will not wait."

"What on earth is wrong with him?" Rosalie wondered to herself as she ushered the black-browed giant into the study.

Meanwhile, the young sinners had gathered in their common room. Only Wanda, Arda and Anne were missing, having early morning practice. The ten were beginning to feel rather apprehensive, now that the first excitement was over. What would Gaudenz say? Would he go to the Head and complain that they had been interfering with his work? In that case, what would she say or do? They were decidedly uneasy, and Kitty put the coping-stone to their discomfort by suddenly suggesting that if Miss Annersley took a dim view of their activities, she might turn them out of the nativity play.

They regarded her with horror.

"Crumpets!" Gillie exclaimed. "I never thought of that! Oh, I do hope you're wrong! I'd hate not to have my part."

"I don't see why she should," Jack said uncomfortably. "We weren't being bad. We only wanted to help Gaudenz."

"Jack—en français, s'il vous plaît!" said Rosamund Lilley, who had come to seek Celia Everett and send her to explain—if she could—just why she had left her dressing gown tossed over her bed instead of hanging it up on its peg. "C'est vendredi, ma petite."

Jack went scarlet and Rosamund, having caught Celia, went off with her.

"Oh, ma pauvre Jack!" Wanda exclaimed. Then: "Mais, Jack! Où vas-tu?"

"Je vais payer mon amende," Jack returned dismally. She had been fined twice already this week for the same thing and this meant that she was now penniless.

"Ça ne fait rien," Renata said soothingly. "Demain, c'est samedi, et alors, tu recevras plus de l'argent."

She went off to drop her centime into the fines box in the entrance hall and came back still looking troubled. However, there was little time for more discussion, for just after she returned, the gong sounded and they had to be silent and march into the Speisesaal for Frühstück.

More than one of them glanced anxiously at the Head when she entered to take her place at the high table. Her face was as tranquil as usual and Kitty, always an optimist, even began to hope that Gaudenz had been so pleased to find he had all that less work to do that he had said nothing about it. Gillie and Jack were not hopeful at all. All they could think was that Gaudenz had not had time as yet to find out what had happened. The other seven hung between these two opinions.

Miss Annersley said Grace and they sat down. Milky coffee, rolls, butter and honey went their usual way. Only the ten seemed to have lost their appetites, for Kitty was becoming influenced by the glum faces of her own gang and had reverted to the idea that perhaps they might lose their parts in the play over this affair. She would hate it if that happened. She had a very nice part with quite a good amount of speaking. Even Wanda, who was merely an angel, felt the same way. Besides, it would be such a disgrace to be out of the play and how could they explain it if any outsider asked questions?

Francie Wilford, the prefect on duty at their table, raised her eyebrows skyhigh when Jack refused a third roll. When Gillie was caught playing with her second, the prefect wondered if she should report them to Matron. She looked round the table. They weren't the only ones by a long chalk. Quite a number of the Lower IVb girls seemed to have lost their appetites. Were they in for an epidemic? How ghastly if they were! Then Francie had another look and decided to wait a little.

"It's my belief," she thought as she placidly buttered her own fifth roll, "that those young imps have been up to something and now they're afraid of consequences. What on earth can they have been doing? Six of ours and four of St Hilda's. And every last one of them a demon! I'll wait."

Frühstück came to an end. Miss Annersley struck her bell twice as a signal that she had some announcement to make, and Francie, her suspicions well aroused, noted that every last one of the ten first went scarlet and then paled. She sat back and waited.

The Head stood up. "One moment, girls," she said, her beautiful voice unusually grave. "I wish to know which girls painted golden syrup over the doors in the passage leading to the kitchens last night?"

There was an electric pause. Most people looked startled, including the criminals themselves, for this was something they had never thought of. One or two people looked horrified, among them Miss Ashley. Quite a number of the younger mistresses and senior girls were hard put to it to stifle their giggles, once the first surprise was over. The next minute, however, a minor sensation came when no fewer than ten Middles got to their feet and stood gazing at the tablecloth, their faces scarlet, as they all said in the meekest tones, "C'est moi, Madame." Then they shut their lips and stood there looking supremely silly.

At sight of her own four pupils, Miss Ashley gave vent to a most peculiar sound. It was neither snort, groan nor cry, but a compound of all. Miss Wilmot, whose sense of humour had got her into trouble at intervals most of her life, dropped her handkerchief and grovelled under the table after it, not coming up until she could control herself again. Several people bit their lips. Even so, all might have been well, but at the very junior table little Carlotta von Ahlen, new that term, exclaimed, "Oh, c'est un loup qui est sous la table!"

That did it! Why Carlotta should have imagined a wolf was in the room, no one knew, but her remark, coming on top of the rest, let loose a gale of laughter. The only people who did not laugh were the ten, and they were far too much overcome by thought of what was going to follow to pay any heed to the foolishness of Carlotta or anyone else; and Miss Ashley herself, who sat bolt upright, looking round resentfully. She saw no cause for laughter!

Miss Annersley touched her bell for silence almost immediately and got it, but there was a suspicious quiver in her voice as she said, "I see." Then she was silent and the ten felt like screaming. However, she went on quite seriously, "When you ten silly little girls have finished

123

your dormitory work, you are to miss your walk and come straight to me in the study."

Their faces fell. It was the first really fine day for more than a week. The high wind, which had dropped now, had dried the mud and already word had gone round that walks might be an hour long instead of the usual thirty minutes. This was the first fruits of their exploit the night before and goodness only knew what else was to come!

Miss Annersley knew exactly what they were feeling. She also knew that presently they would feel the epithet she had applied to them before the entire school and she knew that would hurt as well. She had intended it to. She waited a moment longer to let it sink in before she continued, "Further, you are to speak to nobody until I have seen you—nobody at all. And nobody is to speak to you. Is that understood?"

Everyone said yes, though Miss Ashley felt furious, for it cut the ground from under her feet. She had been meaning to catch her own four and find out all about the affair at the first possible moment. To do her justice, she was chiefly occupied just then with how Miss Holroyd would look at it. She would certainly think that St Hilda's mistresses had failed in their duty when four of their girls could be involved in such a trick.

The Head merely replied, "Thank you. School, stand for Grace, please."

Grace was said, the tables were cleared and everyone hurried upstairs, most of them intent on getting through the dormitory work as fast as they could in order to have longer outside. Only the ten were at all inclined to loiter. However, their dormitory prefects gave them short shrift. They were told to hurry up and Len Maynard went to the length of marshalling her share of the gang and walking them downstairs to the very door of the study. She might not speak to them, but there was sympathy in her eyes when Jack dared to glance up at her. She waited until the rest had assembled and then left them to their doom, only waiting until she was out of hearing to explode into laughter. Of that, however, they knew nothing.

They stood where they were for a moment, their hearts down in their shoes. Even Kitty looked in the depths. She had met Miss Ashley in the corridor and the look she had received from the mistress had ended her volatility for the time being. Ashey, as she reflected, was on the warpath and no mistake.

The rest, meanwhile, were exchanging looks which said plainly as words, "You knock!"

It was Barbara who finally did so, a timid little tap which no one could have heard. Miss Annersley, however, had been warned of their arrival by the sound of their footsteps and she was prepared. She and Rosalie Dene had been enjoying a good laugh over the affair, but at a sign, the secretary skipped into her own room, closing the intercommunicating door, and the Head straightened her face, sat upright, looking very formidable, and called, "Entrez!"

The door of Miss Annersley's study was opened not much more than a crack and they sidled in, one after the other, making themselves as small as they could. Finally, they were standing before the desk in a straight line, all staring at the floor and all crimson again.

The Head regarded them in silence before she spoke. Then she said, "And whose idea was it?"

"Er-mine," Jack faltered after a lengthy pause—not from fear, but because the very blandness of the Head's question had thrown her off balance and she was not very sure what to say. She was at once cried down by her accomplices.

"It wasn't only you! We all helped!" Barbara cried.

"And anyhow, it was me said we'd go and ask Karen if we could have the two Minettes to play with," Kitty put in. "That really began it."

"If you come to that," Jack began, when the Head, who had sat back for a moment, cut in.

"Just a moment, please. Address your remarks to me and not to each other. Now continue, Jack." She spoke in English, for she thought they were all too agitated to understand if she spoke French.

"Well," Jack said, "I really began it, I suppose, 'cos I said we'd—er—we'd stroll round the corridors."

"But," Mary took her share bravely, "it was me saying everything was so dull that started Jack off. So I s'pose it was really me began it."

How she ever contrived to keep a straight face through all this, Miss Annersley could never say. She did it, though, and looked so calmly judicial that suddenly their tongues ceased and they fell silent. She sat still and surveyed them, also in silence, till some of them nearly broke into wild yells.

But before they reached that pitch, she did speak. "I see. Now begin at the beginning, please, Barbara—you are the eldest, aren't you?—and tell me the whole story straight through. The rest of you remain silent. If you have anything to say, I'll hear you when Barbara has finished."

Somehow Barbara got through the story and she told it in much detail. By the time she had ended, Miss Annersley felt she knew it all.

"I see," she said. "It was partly boredom, partly a genuine wish to help Gaudenz, partly—and mostly—sheer mischief. Well, having made such a mess of his work, you will, of course, set it to rights. Tomorrow is Saturday. It is also the prefects' evening. I'm sorry, but none of you will be present at it. Instead, you will spend the time in washing the two doors you messed up thoroughly clean. When the wood is dry, you shall help Gaudenz as you wished. You shall oil and polish them until they look exactly like his work. There will be no free time for any of you until that is done. I except Sunday, of course. You can't hope to finish on Saturday, so that means your free time on Monday as well—and on Tuesday, if it isn't done before. Perhaps that will help you to remember that unpainted woodwork is usually oiled and polished and not varnished. That is your punishment. Now it is growing late and the others will be back shortly. Go to your form room and take out your books for the first two lessons as usual. I'm sorry you have had to miss your morning walk, but if you will do silly things without stopping to think, you must be prepared to pay the penalty. That is all. Run along and try to think in future."

She stood up and ten crestfallen girls went meekly along to Lower IVb to prepare for the first half of the morning's lessons. But, as Jack pointed out with some vigour when they were safely in their form room, at least they were still in the play, so it might have been much worse. They hadn't even been fined or told to give in bad marks. The Head, though none of them knew the expression, had tempered justice with mercy. They must miss the fun of the prefects' evening and lose their free time. Well, that was hard luck but anything was better than being out of the play.

Not one of her fellow criminals disagreed with her.

Chapter 15

MINETTE AGAIN!

WITH the firebrands of Lower IVb all unwontedly subdued—they had not only had to miss the prefects' evening, but all their free time on Monday—and the feud more or less sinking into limbo, those in authority at the Chalet School sat back with long sighs of relief and turned their attention to normal matters.

Three nights a week, they had rehearsals of the various episodes of the nativity play after Abendessen, and on Saturday mornings Mr Denny, the singing master— "Plato" to everyone, though most of them had no idea how the name had originated—arrived for extra carol practice. Various people among the staff spent a good deal of their free time altering costumes from the acting cupboard and making new ones. Miss Yolland and Miss Carey, who were responsible for the art and handcrafts respectively, roped in two other folk to help them and produced an entire new set of haloes and angels' wings.

"Not before time, either!" Miss Ferrars said austerely when she found them at it. "The old ones look as if the two Minettes had bedded down on them for a year!"

News from the Sanatorium about the two patients in whom the school was personally interested continued to be good. Naomi Elton was not only able to move about the wards now, but it was quite clear that the clever doctors and surgeons at the Sanatorium had been able to overcome the terrible deformity left by fire when she was a small girl to such an extent that she was practically straight again and, once she was really strong, would be able to walk without any stick. What was even better, the deformity in her character caused by her injuries was also vanishing. Instead of looking at everything from a morbidly cynical point of view, the Naomi the elder girls visited as often as they were allowed was fast becoming a healthy-minded, happy girl, taking an interest in the things that interest girls in the later teens, and going out to meet people instead of recoiling from them and, as Mary-Lou Trelawney, her greatest friend, had once said, keeping them off with a broomstick.

As for Miss Holroyd, once she had begun to convalesce, she did it by leaps and bounds. It would be months before she was really herself again, for her left arm and shoulder had suffered so severely that there was skin-grafting to be done, and that is a matter of time. But the other burns were healing cleanly. The broken ankle, too, was setting nicely and the doctors all hoped that sooner or later she could cast aside her crutch and stick and even, eventually, walk without a limp at all. She herself had no doubts in the matter. As she told Dr Maynard, she had good healing flesh and an excellent constitution. She was a matter-of-fact, healthy-minded individual and her nerves were righting themselves comfortably. She had roared with laughter over the problem of the two Minettes when they finally broke the news to her, and said that when things had settled down and she was able to get about again, she would go into the matter with Miss Annersley and Miss Wilson. Meantime, she was very pleased to hear that the pair, having begun with a large amount of aversion, were now fast friends.

There could be no question of her being able to go back to work until after the Easter holidays, if then, so St Hilda's was to stay with the Chalet School for the whole of the school year. This would allow time for the building of a new St Hilda's, and this one would be not very far from its present home. In a little village called St Laurenz, some kilometres along the road, had lived a certain Frau Huber whom the school had known well. Frau Huber had died during the previous summer and her chalet with its patch of ground had gone to a nephew who lived much further round the mountain. He wished to sell his legacy and Dr Maynard, hearing of it, had gone to see him on behalf of Miss Holroyd. The result was that Miss Holroyd bought the land and chalet and it was hoped that, as soon as winter was over, a new building, with the old chalet as a nucleus, would arise and be finished in time for St Hilda's to begin work there next autumn.

Quite a number of the girls were thrilled when they heard this. The term had brought Chalet and St Hilda girls together, so that members of both schools were chums. In addition, there was the prospect of matches in tennis, cricket, hockey and netball—even lacrosse, perhaps. Both schools could share in lectures, concerts, and dramatics, and even the annual sale in aid of free beds at the Görnetz Sanatorium. Everyone was thrilled at the prospect—everyone, that is, but Miss Ashley. She still could see no reason why the Chalet School could not give up one of their buildings to St Hilda's until the new one was erected and let them be a separate school again. In vain did Miss Holroyd, as soon as she was well enough, try to drive a little sense into her head. The younger woman stubbornly refused to see how much better it was for the girls that they should have no further disturbance this year.

If she had been honest with herself, Miriam Ashley would have had to own that the main reason for her obstinacy was that, having once been practically senior mistress, she resented having to come down to being a mere ordinary member of staff with no more say in matters than anyone else. However, at that stage, she would not confess it. Miss Kent, whose position she had practically usurped, merely laughed at her, saying that she was quite satisfied with things as they were. She was picking up no end of tips from her present colleagues and having a good time into the bargain. She retailed to her Head quite a few of the ideas she had been taken with, and Miss Holroyd agreed that some, at any rate, of them should be incorporated in St Hilda's arrangements when they were able to open again as a separate school.

"But better not say anything to Miriam Ashley," Miss Holroyd warned her. "She always was inclined to be big-headed and it seems to have grown on her—in this matter, anyhow. She's worse than I ever knew her!"

As for Mrs Thwaites, she had struck up a warm friendship with Matron Lloyd, doyenne of the Chalet School matrons and, to quote herself, sat at that lady's feet, drinking in her words of wisdom. So everyone was pleased and the feud seemed to have come to a natural end, except for Miriam Ashley.

November ended in a thick fog which once more imprisoned everyone who did not need to go out. Then, on December 1st, they woke up to find that a minor blizzard was blowing, with tiny flakes of snow coming whirling down in a regular dervish dance, and those who knew told those who didn't that this snow would lie. The garden was covered with a thick blanket which steadily grew thicker, turning shrubs into the oddest shapes, while the trees began to groan under the weight on their branches. Most of the Juniors spent their free time gazing out of the windows and talking excitedly of snowmen and snowfights. The thoughts of their elders were on skiing and tobogganing.

"If only it goes on lying!" Len Maynard breathed as she and Monica Garstin surveyed the rapidly changing landscape from the window of the prefects' room. "But it's early for it. Usually, we don't have winter sports till next term. However, this is the sort of snow that means business."

"But don't forget that you'll have to wait till it freezes before we can go out in it," her cousin Maeve warned her.

131

"You couldn't ski or toboggan in this. You'd only sink in it. As well you know!"

In actual fact, the snow continued until the Monday evening, when it died away. A harsh wind blowing from the north brought frost and when the girls got up next morning, it was to a world crisp and white and sparkling under the sunbeams straggling through the cloud that was rapidly vanishing.

"Winter sporting today!" Margot Maynard said jubilantly to her own crowd in VIb.

Jean Callendar, of St Hilda's, looked out of the window and shivered ostentatiously. "'Cold' doesn't begin to describe it! I'm none too sure I want to try skiing. I know what learning to skate is like and standing about in this cold will reduce me to a frozen statue!"

"Nonsense!" Margot retorted robustly. "It'll do nothing of the sort. Far otherwise, in fact. By the time you've really got your balance, you'll be begging to shed some of your clothes. Don't do it, by the way. No one will ever agree, so it's waste of energy."

After Frühstück, Miss Annersley told the girls that winter sports were in order that day. There would be no early walk. Instead, as soon as they had attended to dormitory duties, they were to change into skiing suits and come downstairs to Prayers. After Prayers, they would all go to their usual meadow with their skis and toboggans and enjoy a couple of hours in the open air.

"Don't forget your snow-glasses," she ended. "When the sun really comes out, the glare will be dazzling and we don't want any cases of snow blindness."

The Second Prefect, Anna Hoffmann, rose. "Bitte," she asked, "may we, perhaps, our own languages speak while we are out?"

Miss Annersley raised her eyebrows at the staff sitting at the high table and they all nodded. It was usual on the first day of winter sports to make this concession.

Otherwise, a good many of the excited Juniors and Middles would have had fines to pay and quite a number of the Seniors, too.

"You may," the Head said. "But remember that I shall not give permission again this term and also remember that it is only while you are out. In school, you must all try to remember that this is English day. Grace!"

They stood for Grace and then sped round clearing the tables before they hurried upstairs to make their beds, tidy their cubicles and change into their skiing suits. Very trim they all looked in the blue suits with their touches of crimson. The St Hilda girls had none, but Matron had provided enough for everyone. Sticks and snow-glasses were given out and then, booted and skied, they set off, those who were old hands pairing off and taking a novice between them. Some wanted to toboggan, and the elder girls pulled the light toboggans along, skimming over the ground at a speed that made one or two of the St Hilda girls, notably, Monica Garstin, Mary Murrell and all the younger ones look after them enviously.

"I'd love to be able to fly along like that!" Kitty Anderson said as Len Maynard shot past them, drawing a toboggan well laden with small folk, among them her own little sister, Felicity.

"You will before long," Wanda said soothingly. "Jack couldn't do it when she first came, but by the time the snow was over, she could manage quite well. Come with Barbara and me, Kitty, and we'll take you to the meadow."

The time seemed far too short to them when Miss Burnett blew the recall on her whistle, but the Chalet girls, at least, knew better than to argue. St Hilda's girls had also learned that neither grumbling nor coaxing got them anywhere. An odd girl or two complained, but on the whole they went in the most lamblike way and had their reward in hot chocolate when they reached school again.

By the time morning school ended, they all felt that they

had been using unaccustomed muscles and not a few of them murmured together about aching.

"What else do you expect?" Maeve Bettany asked, overhearing a group. "It's the same thing as the first tennis—or any other game, for that matter, when you haven't been doing it for some months. It'll soon wear off; or if it doesn't, go to your matron and she'll give you embrocation."

"I'm aching, all right," said Gillie Garstin, who happened to be one of the crowd near at hand, "but I'd like to have another shot this afternoon, for all that. Do you think they'd let us, Maeve?"

Maeve waved her hand at the nearest window. "In that?" she asked dramatically. "Not a hope, my child! Wait and see what happens tomorrow!" With which she went off to a literature lecture with the Head, while her juniors, having with one accord turned to the window and gasped loudly, realised that there certainly was no hope of going out again that day. The snow had returned and was whirling down so that it was impossible to see anything through it.

The snow continued all that day and well on into the next day; but on the Friday the snow had stopped; the temperature had dropped below zero; and though the sky was still cloudy, Miss Moore, the geography mistress, pronounced it to be merely a cloud mist which would vanish before long. By the time they had settled down to their first lessons of the morning, she proved right. The cloud drew off; the sun came out; and when Break came, they were ordered upstairs to change into skiing kit, and spent a rapturous two hours on the meadow or else flying down the mountain slope to wind up halfway across the meadow on their toboggans. Furthermore, they were allowed to make the most of the fine day by being chased out again as soon as the rest period was over. The radio experts had prophesied fresh snow over the weekend and

Dr Maynard had called in to advise the Head to let the girls take all the advantage they could of the present lull in the weather.

Even the domestic staff were out in their off-times. In fact, the only members of the school who were more or less kept to the house were the two cats. There was always the risk that they might go off and it was much too cold for little pussies to be outside for any length of time.

"It's to be hoped neither of them tries to slip out after dark," Miss Wilmot remarked to her great friend, Miss Ferrars, when Saturday afternoon brought a fresh snowstorm sweeping across the Platz. "If that happened, I'm afraid there'd be one if not two sad little corpses outside next morning."

"Don't worry," Kathy Ferrars returned. "Karen is much too careful to let that happen. I'm positive she'd never go to bed until she was sure those two were safely tucked up in their own place. Or," she added as an after-thought, "let any of us go, either. She'd raise the place for them!"

Neither of them noticed Wanda von Eschenau coming round a corner just in time to overhear this. They went off to their own sitting room and settled down to dresses for the play, since neither was on duty and the girls had begged leave to use the time for extra rehearsals on their own. Lizette Falence was in the song room with some of the soloists, going over their songs; and in Hall, the snowflake ballet was practising hard. Big Monica Caird, who was St Joseph in the final tableau, having nothing to learn herself, had collected the very little ones in the gym and was giving them a good time with oranges and lemons, twos and threes and other games of the kind, with Monica Garstin and Rosamund Lilley to help her. No mistresses were needed, and they obligingly turned their attention to props and dresses, for the time was growing short now.

In the evening, the staff took charge and ran progressive games with tiny prizes and everyone went to bed happy and, it must be admitted, drowsy. At any rate, most of them dropped off to sleep as soon as they had snuggled down, and the rest were not long in following their example.

Just why two of the Middles should have had nightmares, no one could say. The fact remains that Gillie Garstin, who was scarcely awake when she lay down, slept soundly until shortly after midnight when she began to dream. It was a horrific dream of the two Minettes, swollen to the size of tigers and standing one on each side of her, howling at her. At the same time, Jack Lambert, in the next cubicle but one, was also dreaming, even more horrifically. Both tossed and squirmed until their plumeaux landed on the floor with melancholy "Flumps!" and the bitter cold wakened them effectually.

"Gosh!" Jack exclaimed aloud. "Where's—and what—?"

Then she heard a loud gasp telling her that someone else was also awake. She tumbled out of bed, pulled on slippers and dressing gown, made her way down the aisle, peeping into Wanda's cubicle where that young woman was slumbering sweetly, and came to Gillie's. Gillie was also out of bed and struggling with her plumeau, her curly hair standing on end.

Visiting was strictly forbidden, but Jack chose to ignore rules. She slipped in, nearly startling Gillie into a wild yell of surprise, and grinned at her. The snow had ended for the time being, and the full moon was struggling through the light wrack of cloud that still remained in the sky. It was bitterly cold and, even in her thick dressing gown, Jack was shivering. Gillie, who had not bothered with such niceties, looked blue with cold.

"You ass! Put on your gown!" Jack ordered in a mutter. "D'you want to go to San with pneumonia?"

Gillie dropped the plumeau and thankfully reached for her own warm gown.

"Come on! I'll give you a hand with this," Jack went on in the same mutter. "Then you can come and help me with mine. *Hup* she comes!"

Between them, they heaved up the plumeau and then attended to Jack's. That would have been all right and no one could have blamed them for helping each other. But both were wide awake now and it seemed good to Jack to suggest that they should pop out into the corridor where they might open a window and take a look at the scene. Their own windows were covered with frost patterns.

Gillie was nothing loth. They pattered out, still without rousing anyone else, and made their way to the big casement at the far end of the corridor. This they pushed open cautiously and both gasped again as the icy air caught them. For all that, they leaned out and gazed admiringly at the scene—for exactly two seconds. At that very moment, their sharp ears heard a sad little wail which there was no mistaking.

"Minette!" they exclaimed together.

"She's out there in all this bitter cold!" Gillie added. "What shall we do?"

As they were later told with a good deal of severity, what they should have done was to go and report to their dormitory prefect—Len Maynard. She would have gone to Matron. What they did do was to resolve to rescue their pet themselves. Wanda had duly reported what she had overheard and the thought of poor little Minette being a corpse by the morning was too much for any common sense they might have, especially when another wail, even more pitiful, reached them.

"Come on!" Jack said. "We'll get her in pronto! She's on the roof, though goodness knows how she got there. We must put on a few clothes and then we'll have a shot. I know how we can get up. Scram!"

Chapter 16

The Rescue

The sinful pair tiptoed back to their cubicles and pulled on their clothes as fast as they could. Jack added a thick pullover and her Sunday coat to her usual attire. Footwear was a problem. She rather thought they ought to have their nailed boots on, but that would mean going downstairs to fetch them and probably waking someone. Even if they did manage to get to the Splashery and back, the noise of their steps on the polished floors would certainly do it.

"Have to make it plims," she muttered to herself. "Mine are up here for new laces. I hope Gillie's are, too."

She fished out her plimsolls and put them on, tying the laces in tight knots. A thick woolly scarf was tied round her head and she had an old pair of woolly mitts into which she could tuck her hands. That done, she stole along to Gillie's cubicle and found her partner in crime just ready. They left the dormitory and Jack led the way to the trunk room. This was a long, narrow room running under the eaves of the building. It had two casement windows, each opening at only the one side. There was also a skylight, and her first idea had been to get out through that. However, they found it impossible to open with the weight of snow on it. They must use one of the casements.

These were dormers, set on the roof, so that it would be easy enough to get out. The difficulty would be to find Minette and then, if she were not fairly near, to get hold of her.

As soon as they were safely in the trunk room, Jack explained her ideas to Gillie, who was quite ready to fall

138

in with them. They lifted one of the trunks and set it firmly on top of the one beneath the window. Another gave them a step up. That done, they pushed open the casement and leaned out.

The school had chimney stacks at either end of the main building, relics of the time when it had been a guest house and wood fires had been burned in the stoves. Now, only one group was in use for the furnaces which kept the central heating going. By dint of leaning far out, they were able to locate Minette, huddled up against this one. Both girls tried calling her, but she was terrified and almost rigid with cold into the bargain. She mewed pathetically at them, but she refused to budge. "We'll just have to go after her," Gillie said. "She's St Hilda's cat, really, so I'd better be the one. You hang on here and be ready to grab her when I get back with her."

"You don't know which she is!" Jack retorted. "She may quite well be the one Len and Wanda brought back by mistake. Anyhow, I'm more accustomed to skating about on frozen snow than you are, so it ought to be me. And I say! We'd better put our plims on under our socks to give us more grip. But I do wish she'd come for calling. Cats are such sure-footed beasts."

She thrust her black head out of the window and called again, this time with no caution whatsoever. It was no use. Minette was not moving for anyone.

From the floor, where she was obeying Jack's suggestion, Gillie looked up to say, "P'raps we'd better both go. It may need us both."

"OK. Half a tick till I change my socks and plims." And Jack plumped down on the floor and set to work.

Ready at last, they both climbed on to the trunks and gazed out.

"I'll go first," Jack said. "Hang on to my wrist till I get on to the roof and then I'll give you a hand up. Only, whatever you do, move slowly and carefully. We can't rush at a thing like this." Which was a good deal more common sense than anyone would have expected such a madcap to show.

If there had been any older person to see their gyrations, she would almost inevitably have suffered heart failure. However, both were agile enough and both had good heads for heights. They were out on the roof at last and then Jack gave a muffled whoop of triumph as she pointed to the ridged lines that ran from side to side.

"Look at those! I'd forgotten the stones. They'll give us quite a decent foothold. This won't be too hard. The only thing to remember is to go carefully and never to look down. Keep looking straight ahead."

"How are we doing it?" Gillie asked as Jack began to move cautiously upwards.

"Up to the ridge and sit astride and then we can shuffle along it. Come on!"

Just how they managed it, no one ever knew—not even themselves. Somehow they got up that icy slope and reached the ridge-pole. Once there, they felt comparatively safe, if chilly. They sat astride it and began inching their way carefully along it, both keeping their eyes rigidly on the chimney stack where Minette was howling like a banshee.

"Poor Minette!" Jack called. "We're coming! We'll soon have you out of this! Keep going, Gillie! We're getting along."

Minette gave vent to a yowl which rang through the frosty air, beating all her former efforts into a cocked hat. It pierced the somewhat uneasy slumbers of Miss Ashley, who had her window open the merest crack. Like Jack and Gillie, she had been dreaming and Minette's squall reached her. She sat up in bed in time to hear still another, and was out on the floor and switching on her light in short order. Just where the cries came from, she had no idea as yet, but she must do something about it. She huddled on slippers and gown and opened her door. Only the pilot-lights were on, but they were enough to show her the corridor, bare of anything like a cat. She shot back to her room, pushed the window wide and hung out, searching the snow-covered ground with anxious eyes; but there was nothing alive out there. Then another long-drawn-out "Mia-o-u!" dropped from above and she knew where the cat was.

"Oh, heavens!" she thought as she frantically pulled on a few clothes. "How on earth can I get at her? Better go up and see if I can coax her to come to me at one of the windows. If not, I don't know what I'm going to do. Try to reach her somehow, I hope. It won't be too easy. Thank goodness for a full moon! At least I shall be able to see what I'm doing!"

By this time she was hurrying up the stairs to the top floor. At once her eye was caught by the light coming from the boxroom door which the girls had left ajar. She made for it, peered in and saw the casement flung open to its widest extent.

"So that's how she got out there!" she thought—quite wrongly—as she made her way between the piles of trunks and cases, clambered on the erection the two had left, and looked out.

She saw Minette against the chimney stack. She also saw two humped-up figures moving very slowly along the ridge, and nearly fell off her perch with horror. She had no idea who they were, but that they were girls was plain enough. Now what was she to do? She dared not utter a sound in case she startled them and made them lose their balance. Neither did she dare to leave them to seek help though how she could assist them if either slipped, she had not the faintest idea. At least she must wait until they had reached the stack. That would give them a much better hand hold than the ridge and then perhaps she could venture to call to them to stay where they were till help came. Meanwhile, now that her human friends were at hand, Minette was shrieking her woes to high heaven in a way that should have roused the sleepers at Freudesheim, let alone those in the school.

Poor Miriam Ashley watched, spellbound, as the first of the figures straddling the ridge finally reached the stack and clutched the frantic cat with one hand while, with the other, she held on to the stack itself. A clarion voice proclaimed, "Got her!" Then, in different tones, "Oh gosh! She's soot from here to yonder! She must have been chimney climbing! Hi! Chuck it, Minette! You're all right now! Gillie, I daren't try to pass her to you. She's kicking and clawing like mad. You get back and I'll follow when I've got her safe."

Jack Lambert and Gillie Garstin!

"When I get hold of them safely!" Miss Ashley thought vengefully.

But there was a pause and it was all Miss Ashley could do to keep herself from screaming. Clinging with knees and feet, Jack had taken her free hand off the stack and was pulling the scarf from her head. Somehow, she managed to imprison Minette in it, winding it round her and tying it firmly. Minette squalled louder than ever, but Jack made sure of her. Minette could neither kick nor scratch in her cocoon-like windings. Jack finished by securing the shrieking bundle round her waist. Then she dropped her hands to the ridge.

"Are you on the way, Gill?" she called.

"Yes!" Gillie replied, most untruthfully, for she had stayed where she was until she was sure her leader was ready to move. However, she began to back slowly, followed by Jack while Miss Ashley, realising fully what was meant by having one's heart in one's mouth, watched agonisedly.

Meanwhile, between the yells of the cat and the yells of the girls, Matey had wakened. It took her less than one minute to realise that the noise came from overhead. In three more, she was tearing up the stairs to the top floor. She saw the light streaming from the trunk-room doorway and made straight for it. What she saw told her that the cat, at least, was on the roof. She dived straight for the window. Miriam Ashley heard her and turned—and it was not the moonlight that made her look deathly white.

"Matron!" she gasped. "Oh, thank God someone's come! Gillie Garstin and Jack Lambert are out there on the roof, rescuing Minette. I daren't make a sound in case I startled them and—and—I think I'm going to be sick!"

"Not this minute you aren't!" Matron promptly took charge. "Get down from there and go and fetch Nancy Wilmot as fast as you can. Quick!"

Miss Ashley gulped, but she did as she was told while Matron took her place, thrust out her head and stared anxiously at the antics going on on the ridge of the roof. Gillie was backing carefully along it towards the window and Jack was following her at a much slower rate. Minette was immobilised for the moment, but she was not a lightweight and her yowling was enough to bewilder someone much older than Jack.

Watching them and feeling sick enough herself, Matron knew that the real difficulty would come when they had to leave the ridge and get down the icy slope to the window itself. Like Jack, she had seen the long lines of heavy stones, securely roped to the roof, and she knew that they would give the girls a fighting chance. Even so, she could not imagine how they could possibly negotiate that steep pitch; and, if they fell, the ground below was like iron. Then she heard the sound of scurrying feet and the next moment Nancy Wilmot of the long arms, powerful shoulders and six feet of height was beside her.

"What's cooking?" she demanded as she mounted beside Matey.

143

She thrust out her head, as she spoke. She gave a gasp, but she said nothing. The situation on the roof was too delicate for that.

Slowly, slowly—maddeningly so to the watchers at the windows (Miss Ashley had gone to the other and was staring at what she could see)—Gillie and Jack edged their way backwards till they were almost over the first casement. There, Gillie stopped and halted her friend.

"Woa, Jack! We're bang on to the window. What now?"

"We get down to it, of course." Jack's voice was quite matter-of-fact. "Now listen carefully, Gillie. Can you reach down to the first stone, d'you think? Be careful! For mercy's sake don't overbalance. And don't look down. Feel for it with your foot. It's there all right."

Gillie fumbled a moment. "Yes, I've got it. No stretch at all."

"Good! Get your leg back and bring the other over. Hang on to the ridge!"

Gillie carefully drew her off leg across and then, clinging to the ridge, she extended the other and planted it against the stone. "I've got it. But how will you manage with Minette?"

"I'll manage somehow. I'll worry about that in a moment," Jack said airily. "You hang on and see if you can get your foot down to the rock below. Steady does it!"

Miss Ashley nearly screamed aloud at this and Matron stiffened. Miss Wilmot, leaning out at a dangerous angle, prepared to do her best to catch Gillie's clothes if she slipped. But nothing happened. The guardian angels of the pair must certainly have been working overtime that night. Gillie got her foot somehow to the second row of rocks, slid one hand down to clutch at the first and reached down to the third and last with her free foot.

Nancy Wilmot waited until she seemed to be safe. Then, speaking very quietly, she said, "It's all right, Gillie. I'm here and I'll help you. Stretch down to the gutter and I'll get your arm. Take your time. You're quite safe now."

Gillie said later that she had no idea who was speaking. She did as she was told, and two minutes later she was hauled through the window and dropped on the floor into the arms of Miss Ashley who had left her stance and came just in time to catch her. Gillie was shaking, whether with cold or fear no one had any time just then to find out. Jack had still to be brought to safety and, burdened as she was by Minette, it was going to be more difficult.

Miss Wilmot turned her head and called Gillie. "Gillie, come here and call to Jack and tell her you're safe. Then tell her she is to stay where she is for a moment. I'm going up myself to help her. Speak in your usual tone."

Somewhat shakily, Gillie gave the message before she slid down to the lower trunk, whence Miss Ashley picked her up and carried her out of the way. Nancy Wilmot, having surveyed her terrain and thanked her stars that, urged by Mlle de Lachennais, a keen alpiniste, she had done a fair amount of mountain climbing, got out of the window and, with her great height and long arms, was speedily holding Jack, who was nearly at the end of her tether.

"All right, Jack; cling on another moment or two and I'll have you safely home. Where's that cat? There?" as Jack nodded towards her burden, which was silent, having evidently exhausted herself at last. "Good! Now then!"

It was tricky going for the next moment or two and Miss Ashley, who had joined Matron on the trunk, felt sick all over again. But she bit her lips and steadied herself. Thanks to that, Jack was got safely through the casement and dropped on the floor. Miss Wilmot contrived to reach her goal without too much difficulty and then she too was inside and Matron, with a shudder, was slamming the window shut and latching it securely. She got down from the trunks with shaking legs and sat down on the nearest trunk, breathing hard.

Jack brought her out of that. "Pup-please, will someone undo Minette?" she asked tremulously. "I—I think—she—she's fainted."

Minette herself put an end to that idea by lifting up her voice in a weak but definite, "Me-ew!" and Miss Wilmot, steady again, came to undo the knots and unroll Minette. She finished and set the poor cat on her feet. Minette promptly rolled over on her side, and that finished Gillie who was watching. She burst into tears. Jack was infected at once and the pair of them howled like a couple of babies.

"Now that's enough," Matey said, herself once more. "Stop making that silly noise, both of you. Do you want to wake up the entire school? Come along to San and we'll get Nurse to attend to you. Did you hear what I said?" as they still roared. "Stop it at once—bawling like a pair of infants! I'm ashamed of you!"

But the two mistresses noticed that her usual fresh colour was missing and she looked years older from the strain. Nancy Wilmot picked up Jack. Giving her a slight shake, she said severely, "Stop it, Jack! Stop it at once!"

Jack gave a fearful gulp, but she managed to get hold of herself and Miriam Ashley, treating Gillie the same way, hushed her sobs. Matron left them and headed for the school sanatorium to wake Nurse and help her prepare. Miss Ashley stooped as she led Gillie from the trunk room with an arm round her to support her, and scooped Minette up in her free arm.

"Minette's all right," she said, hoping to calm the pair a little. "I expect she's stiff with the cold and being bundled up like that, poor little beast. We'll ask Nurse for hot milk for her and then she'll be all right. Come along, Gillie, and stop crying."

Choking down their sobs, they stopped crying and were hustled downstairs, where Nurse was ready for them. She had turned on two baths and when they came out of them, they were scrubbed down with hot towels, put into pyjamas warm from the airing cupboard, dosed with Nurse's favourite nostrum of hot milk and treacle and tucked up between blankets, after which, what with their exertions, their very mixed emotions, and the treatment they had just undergone, they were asleep almost at once. Meanwhile Miss Wilmot made coffee for themselves, and Miss Ashley, helping herself to one of Nurse's towels, rubbed Minette, who was black with soot, and got the worst of it off. She commandeered some of the hot milk and coaxed her to drink it, after which she carried the lady downstairs to the kitchens and tucked her in bed beside her pair who was lying in the big basket they shared, curled up in a fat, tabby ball. Minette made no objection. She, too, was worn out. By the time Miriam got back to the San, the coffee was ready and she accepted her cupful thankfully.

"And now, what has all this been in aid of?" Nurse asked chattily.

Matron was not in a chatty mood and she suppressed her at once. "You'll hear all about it tomorrow. Just now, we are all going back to bed and I, for one, shall be thankful to get there. I only hope I don't have a nightmare after this experience! Come along, you two, Nancy and Miriam! It's two o'clock in the morning and if you don't want your sleep, I do."

She paused to go and look at the sleepers in the beds, but both were fathoms deep and never stirred. Miss Wilmot got up from the chair in which she had been lounging, and pulled Miriam Ashley to her feet. "Come on, Mirrie! You've been here long enough to know that Matey is the original She-who-must-be-obeyed! Bed for everyone, and pronto at that!" And with an arm tucked through that of Miriam Ashley who was dazedly realising that she was no longer an outsider at the Chalet School, but truly one of them as long as St Hilda's was there, she bade Nurse and Matron goodnight and went off with her.

The feud, at long last, was over!

Chapter 17

The End of it All

Nemesis should have descended on Jack and Gillie next day, but next day found the pair of them still in San with the beginning of violent colds. Matey always flatly refused to have infectious colds in the school, so Nurse kept them firmly quarantined until the worst was over and they were able to be up and about with noses and eyes looking normal and all sneezing and sniffing at an end.

Miss Annersley, who had received a horrid shock when she heard of their exploits on the roof, visited them that first day, but she said very little. In fact, having regard to their streaming eyes and noses, aches and shivers and their inclination to tears, the result of reaction from the strain they had undergone, all she did say was that she would have a talk with them when they were well again. Meantime, she was sure they would be glad to know that Minette seemed none the worse for her adventure and had demolished her usual good breakfast. Then she left them to Nurse, and for six long days they saw no one else.

"Whad d'you thi'g they will do to us?" Gillie asked on the third day.

"I do'd dow," Jack replied with equal thickness. "I hope it wo'd beed losi'g our parts id the play!" She wound up with a mighty sneeze.

When they finally waited on the Head, she gave them a dressing-down she had never bettered, but said nothing about the play. Not that they escaped scot-free. For the remainder of the term, they would not sleep in their cubicles because, she told them, they were clearly not to be trusted. They would remain in San in two of the little rooms opening off the main ward. Nurse would keep an eye on them, and only if she had good reports to give of them would they be allowed to return to their dormitory next term.

Neither wept, but neither felt happy. To be told that they were untrustworthy was a nasty blow and one they took quite two days to recover from.

Joey Maynard chuckled when she heard the whole story. "Well, that should sort them!" she commented. "Little wretches! All the same, Hilda, it's quite an idea for my next school yarn."

"I'd prefer them not to give you ideas for your school yarns if it means their going to lengths of that kind!" Miss Annersley retorted. "I feel sick whenever I think of the risks they took!"

"But how on earth did Minette get there in the first place?" Joey demanded. "It couldn't have been through any window from what you and Matey say, so how did she do it, since cats don't have wings?"

"Oh, we've solved that," her friend told her. "The furnaces were not drawing properly, so Gaudenz opened the doors of those we don't use to see if there was any stoppage there. Minette must have slipped in when no one was looking. It would be easy enough for a cat to scramble up. That accounts for the fact that she was black with soot when she was got in. What I still don't know and never shall is how on earth she got out of the chimney and down to the roof without falling. She would certainly have been killed if she had done so."

"Oh, cats have nine lives—though I don't know I'd advise any cat to experiment that way," Joey returned with another chuckle.

It was a thoroughly subdued pair that finally came back into school. For the whole of that week they sang very small and did their best to keep in the background. After that, their natural exuberance asserted itself, rather to the relief of their elders. A meek and humble Jack and Gillie was so unusual as to make people worry about the effect of the exploit on their nerves. In any case, by that time the school was in the thick of final rehearsals for the play and no one had much time to think of anything else. When they were not having lessons or walks—the snow and frost had gone during their quarantine period—they were either rehearsing the various scenes or practising carols. The final dress rehearsal was a terrible affair, when very few seemed to know their lines. The prettiest dance was ruined by two small people getting bad attacks of stagefright, losing their places in the figures and putting out everyone else. The choir seemed incapable of singing anything but flat. Finally, the scene-shifters muddled up two of the scenes and the lavish Charles I scene had to be played against Puritan severity with startling results.

"Oh well, I'd rather have a bad last rehearsal and a decent performance on the day than the other way round," Miss Kent said consolingly to Miss Ferrars, who looked ready to tear her hair before the fiasco came to an end. "Buck up, Kathy! It'll be all right tomorrow, you'll see!"

"It certainly couldn't be any worse," the producer returned in melancholy tones. "I know they always say a bad last rehearsal means a good show, but honestly!"

The morning of the day itself was spent in conveying various properties, forgotten the day before, to St Luke's Hall. This was a very complete building presented to the great Sanatorium by the joint efforts of sundry grateful people. It had an auditorium capable of seating four hundred people and a good-sized stage.

The ticket office on this occasion was in the charge of members of St Mildred's, who were also responsible for refreshments and programmes. Next term, when the finishing branch would produce its annual pantomime, the school proper would see to that in its turn. Mr

Denny was conductor of the orchestra, which was supplied by members from both branches, and one of the mistresses took over the piano when necessary.

"I wish there was time for just one more rehearsal!" sighed Miss Charlesworth, who was in charge of the Charles I episode and none too happy about her performers after yesterday's affair. "I suppose we couldn't have just one quick run through this morning?"

"Not even the merest sniff of one," Miss Ferrars assured her. "We stand or fall by all we've done, now. The girls are to have a good, brisk walk home and by the time we get there, it'll be time for Mittagessen or Karen and Co. will be late for the show. You stop nattering and come along! We've done our best and any more rehearsals would just make the whole crowd so jittery, I doubt if they'd put up any sort of a show. Come along!"

In fact, by the time they were all assembled in the dressing rooms, there was no chance for anyone to feel nervous. The Juniors had to be kept in order and though as many people as possible dressed in the dormitories, it was impossible to have angels with soaring wings crowding into the coaches which bore them to the opposite end of the Platz. Some of the other dresses were also better donned at the hall, and there was generally extra touching-up to do to make-up and hair.

Rosamund Lilley, playing the Blessed Virgin, dressed swiftly and then joined Len Maynard who, as the Puritan Father, had dressed at school and was now on the stage, looking through a peephole in the curtains. Early as it was, two or three people were already coming in to take their seats, and since as many Old Girls as possible always turned up for the plays, anyone who could was expected to look out for them and report when she could to the rest.

"Mary-Lou and Verity have arrived," she said in low tones as Rosamund joined her. "And they have Naomi with them, too. I knew they were coming. Auntie

Doris—Mary-Lou's mother—has come out for the winter. She's staying at Unter den Kiefern down below. Oh, here's Mamma coming along with Cecil. I suppose the twins are in the cloakroom having their naps. I can see both Anna and Rösli at the back."

"There's Vi Lucy with Betsy," Rosamund added excitedly. "I didn't know Betsy was coming. Oh, and look, Len! There's Mme Courvoisier!"

"I can see Tante Marie," reported Wanda von Eschenau who, as one of the angels, had been dressed and sent on the stage out of the way with two or three others. "She's just come in with Tante Frieda. They're going to sit with Aunt Joey."

"Hush!" Len said. "If you squeak like that, you'll be heard all over!"

Wanda subsided and Rosamund murmured, "Naomi looks piles better, doesn't she? But how grown-up Verity looks!"

Len nodded and turned away. "We'd better give up now. They're sending all those baby angels on and if they see us peeping, they'll want to have a go themselves. Wanda, go to the others now. You've been at the curtains long enough. Here come the big angels and the archangels. It must be nearly time for the orchestra."

"And here's Miss Burnett and Miss Ashley," Rosamund added in the same subdued tones. "Time we went, Len."

The two big girls left the stage and the mistresses, responsible for this opening scene, got their performers into their places, while from the wings came a peremptory order, "Clear the stage" in Miss Ferrars' voice. Beneath the edge of the curtains gleamed the footlights and clapping sounded as a sign that the orchestra were taking their places. It swelled up louder as Mr Denny climbed into the conductor's rostrum. One minute later, the orchestra broke into an arrangement of Bach's "Jesu, Joy

152

of Man's Desiring". The last beautiful note died away into silence. Then came the chords of a gay carol and the curtains swung back on the first episode.

Crowds of tiny angels danced in rings, singing the old Dutch carol, "Christ Jesus Hath a Garden" to a setting composed by Mr Denny—a merry dancing tune. Larger angels came pouring in as the carol ended. They were dressed in robes of green and scarlet and blue, making a lovely contrast with the white and pink and pale blue of the tinies. All the wings were silver or gold and the gaiety and beauty of the scene held the audience spellbound until the last of the carol died away. The rings broke and swung back so that the stage was crowded with angels and archangels, standing with arms and heads uplifted. Then a tall archangel, with red-gold curls framing her face beneath the golden halo on her head, came forward and all turned to hear the news sung.

Margot Maynard possessed a lovely soprano and the carol, written by her sister Con and set by Mr Denny, brought tidings that God in His pity for man had sent His Son to earth as Man and He might save His Creatures from sin and its consequence. Christ was born that night, a Baby, the Child of a pure Maiden, and there was joy sung to earth and joy in Heaven.

At once the baby angels clapped their hands, laughing merrily—Margot had turned her back to the audience and no one saw the awful face she pulled to make that laugh natural—as they once more formed into their dancing rings and whirled round, singing "Gloria in excelsis Deo". All the girls knew that the joyous air to which they sang it was the work of one of the Old Girls, Nina Rutherford, who was already making a name for herself as a concert pianist and who was to make herself an even greater one by her compositions as the years went on.

The curtains fell and the scene-shifters rushed to their work. A backcloth showing a midnight sky with the dark outlines of hills was dropped, and against this were posed shepherds, all looking eagerly towards one corner where the archangels, mounted on staging in tiers of brilliant colours, sang the old English carol "In the Fields with their Flocks Abiding". The curtains were drawn back and the audience gazed thrilled on the beautiful tableau. When the curtains went up again, a banqueting hall in the Middle Ages was revealed, with a crowd of merry boys bringing in the yule log, proudly ridden by small Felix Maynard. The lord and lady of the manor were there with their family and servants about them. There were seats to spare, but when one of the children pointed this out, the lord replied that those were for the Christ-guests. Any who chose to ask for shelter and food that night was welcome in the name of Christ who was born in a stable because there was no room in the inn.

The first to come was a beggar in rags. A group of gleemen and tumblers followed—how Gillie enjoyed turning somersaults and walking on her hands!—and finally a man, a woman and their children who had been benighted on the road. They were all made welcome and as they sat down, the choir sang "Dunkelt im Nacht", an old German carol. The butler came, bringing the wassail bowl and the curtains shut out a delightful scene.

The next tableau showed the three kings pressing on after the star. One bore a glittering crown; one a box which glistened with glass jewels; the third swung a censer from which the blue smoke curled sweetly and slowly. The Austrian carol, "Drei Königen", was sung during this, and almost as soon as the curtains had fallen, they were swept back again to show a merry Christmas in the days of Charles I, with holly and ivy decking the scene. The talk was of the service in church. A stately sarabande and a jolly coranto were danced and the scene ended with everyone singing a Latin carol, "Laus Deo".

Once more the curtain fell and when it rose again, oh, what a change!

It rose on an obvious Puritan home. Gone were the Christmas trappings of holly and ivy. Gone the fine tablecloth and the great dishes. The family here were supping from wooden bowls. They sat on stools and the table was uncovered. Conspicuous on the wall hung a birch rod. Everyone was in the plainest of clothes of the Puritan kind.

One of the children complained of the dull food and was instantly bidden to leave the table and go without any more. Another said discontentedly that he had heard that formerly at Christmas time people had eaten pies stuffed with sugar and fruit and spices and why could they not have the same now?

He was also sent from the table. A girl then said that the Bible said Christmas was a time of gladness, but there was no gladness to be had nowadays.

The father rose up in wrath, his wife bleating agreement with all his remarks. He said that Christmas was an idolatrous custom and should not be celebrated in his house and family. But since his children complained that the day was dull, he would liven it up for them. He reached for the birch rod and they all fled from the room in terror, he after them. From behind the scenes came telltale sounds, blows and shrieks. Then the stern parent brought the three in, bade them kneel and ask their mother's pardon for speaking as they had of the good food she had provided and ended up by making each of the weeping three—they were all bawling at nicely judged intervals—kiss the rod, after which he banished them to their bed chambers, the girl with a task of spinning to perform and the boys with several chapters of a book called *The Youthful Sinner: or The Fair Way to bring up a Child* to learn by heart.

The audience roared over this scene, but were speedily hushed as the choir broke into the old Latin carol "Jubilate Fratres", which swelled out triumphantly.

The tableau which followed this was of Hans Andersen's beautiful story "The Little Matchgirl". Kitty Anderson was the little girl, crouched up against the backcloth which showed a picture of a family round the Christmas tree. Standing behind her was a great archangel with outstretched hands, ready to carry her soul to Heaven. From behind the scenes, the choir sang "Rataplan", the quaint old Provençal carol.

The last episode was of modern times, with children having so much they were not sure what present to look at first. Talk of Christmas pudding and turkey; pantomimes and parties went round. Suddenly, the choir broke into the beloved old German carol "Stille Nacht, Heilige Nacht". The eager chattering ceased. Someone spoke of those who kept no Christmas for they were too poor. There was talk of refugees, the people who had lost their nationalities, and the camps where they had to live, many of them without hope. Someone suggested that gifts might be sent to these folk. Another said, looking round not only the stage audience, but the audience in the auditorium, "Let us remember them with gifts from our plenty." Everyone began to give—a grown-up girl brought woollies; a young man produced a big coat. The children offered toys and someone brought a bowl and handed it round for contributions for food for the starving and destitute.

Maeve Bettany, in her part as mother of the household, came to the front and spoke directly to the audience.

"You have bought tickets for our play and we are grateful for your generosity to our Sanatorium and the sick. Will you extend this generosity, you who expect a joyous Christmastide? When our play ends and as you go out, will you put one coin, however small, in the bowls set at the doors, so that we may send from all here money to provide food for Christmas Day for some, at least, of the starving to whom Christ came as He came to us? Will you?"

The curtain fell on her last word and when it rose, it was to show black curtains against which was set a Christmas crib with people kneeling at it and candles burning before it. At the same time, from behind the scenes rose the strains of Gounod's Christmas song, "Nazareth".

Once more the curtains closed and when they opened for the last time, it was on the scene of the First Christmas. It was all there—the stable with racks of hay for the beasts, the manger filled with straw in which lay the Bambino the school had for these plays, Rosamund as the Madonna, bending over it, Monica Caird, the St Joseph, standing behind her with lantern and staff. All round knelt the people from the different episodes. Behind them ranged the angels and archangels. The triumphant strains of the "Adeste" filled the hall, and everyone sang it with full throats and full hearts.

The curtains fell for the last time as it ended, but as the audience quietly left the hall, there came the sound of coins tinkling and jingling into the bowls placed in readiness for them, and when the girls counted their contents later that evening, it was to find that they had a goodly sum to send to those who might have had no Christmas feasting, but who would now know at least one day when the joy of Christ's Birth came to them.

Miss Holroyd, who had attended the play, turned to Miss Annersley and Miss Wilson who were standing near with several of the mistresses behind them.

"I'm glad," she said soberly, "that my first outing has been to this play. And I am very glad that our girls have been able to take part in it with yours."

"Thank you," Miss Annersley said. "We are glad, too."

But after all, it was Miriam Ashley herself, talking later on to her Head, who summed it up. "I see now how stupid and wrong I've been. You mayn't believe it, but I'm glad we joined the Chalet School. You see, I've learnt that they teach something to the girls besides just lessons—the

157

way to live with other folk and for other folk. Yes; I'm glad of it all. I hope I'll never be such a pigheaded ass again."

But when Joey Maynard heard of it from her Christmas visitor during the holidays, she only nodded and said, "That's the best tribute of all. And exactly what we of the Chalet School all try to do."

Here are some of the most recent titles in our exciting fiction series:

☐ Pursuit of the Deadly Diamonds *J. J. Fortune* £1.25

☐ A Leader in the Chalet School *Elinor M. Brent-Dyer* £1.50

☐ Voyage of Terror *J. H. Brennan* £1.75

☐ The Witch Tree Symbol *Carolyn Keene* £1.50

☐ The Clue in the Broken Blade *Franklin W. Dixon* £1.25

☐ The Mystery of the Purple Pirate *William Arden* £1.25

☐ Chestnut Gold *Patricia Leitch* £1.25

☐ Monsters of the Marsh *David Tant* £1.75

Armadas are available in bookshops and newsagents, but can also be ordered by post.

HOW TO ORDER
ARMADA BOOKS, Cash Sales Dept., GPO Box 29, Douglas, Isle of Man, British Isles. Please send purchase price plus 15p per book (maximum postal charge £3.00). Customers outside the UK also send purchase price plus 15p per book. Cheque, postal or money order — no currency.

NAME (Block letters) _____

ADDRESS _____

_____

_____

ks 1a